MW01594920

A Collection of Short Stories
by
Karen Davis-Pritchett

Dedicated to Team Karen

My Lessons, My Life, My Lifters and My Loves
Philippians 4:13

I am thankful for the gift of writing. This has been a labor of love for many, many, years. Life has a way of making you put your dreams on the shelf and too many times they stay there. So, this process started back in 2002, then, I put it on the shelf. A year ago, after much prayer and contemplation, I started the process over and now it is complete. I used the format of short stories because we are busy. Short stories allow you to steal away for a few minutes. I have always loved short stories and I hope after reading my collection you will share this love with me.

This book was my chaser, finding the energy and the stamina to write, edit, critique, and publish. The picture below is a picture that I captured while on the West Coast in California. It embodies beauty and power, just like the countless women I have met. When I am running too fast and I am depleted and exhausted, I find rest in the sunrise and sunset. It reminds me that there is One greater than I am, and then I can slow down.

I am grateful to God for His faithfulness. I am thankful for the continual support of those that wear the jersey, Team Karen. Special thanks my husband Rev. Pritchett, my amazing parents, my son J3, Kristi and my Sister Cousins. It is because of you that I can dream, reach and acquire.

Love & Hugs,
Karen

Cross Roads Introduction

Women, we find ourselves making decisions every single day. Some of those decisions can have a ripple impact and change our families, careers, health and future in ways we can't even imagine. We stand many times at a crossroad. Trying to decide which way to go. We stand in these crossroad moments alone. Thinking, which way do I turn or do I simply stand here stuck, in the comfort of indecisive nothingness. Sometimes we choose the path that will demand that we run feverishly after people, goals, acceptance, ideas, careers and even that L word, love. We fix our gaze on it and lace up our shoes and take off! Other times we choose the path that will scorch our soul, self-esteem, morals and dreams. We ignore the charred smell and continue to walk along, broken, hurting, dazed and complicit. Some are consumed by the chase, using every resource that they have acquired and every cell of energy to capture that elusive thing. Many become blinded and are only guided by their emotions and flesh, instead of their spirit, as they ignore that a crossroad exists and there is a choice to be made.

Welcome to the crossroad moments of these women…their stories told in their voices. Let's experience their tears, bruises, smiles, messes and exhaustion. What is the prize at the end? Who are the winners? Will the struggles erase their radiance or make it brighter? Should they choose left, or right? What is the cost of the choice and do they have enough capital to pay?

Many questions to be answered as they stand at The Crossroad waiting to Cross a Road.
KDP

Table of Contents

"Susan"

The blue numbers from the clock illuminate the room, then the number slowly changes. This night will last forever; actually, it's morning, 2:45 AM. Then, what seems like an hour later, the time changes to 2:46 AM. I can't believe this is happening again. I feel the anger tighten my chest, as sleep eludes me. I can't sleep, even though I am exhausted.

Okay Susan, get a grip, you need to go to sleep and deal with this later. Hmm, how can I sleep when I have no clue where my husband is? I have left at least 10 messages on his cell and at least 20 texts; he still hasn't responded.

My mind is filled with the words that I will hurl at him when he walks through the door, if he ever walks through the door. I imagine the conversation and think of what his answers will be, so I will be ready to retaliate. Everything seems to be a blur and is getting all mixed up in my head. My stomach feels a little queasy. Geesh, I do not feel well.

Easing out of bed, I make my way to the bathroom. I need to get some sleep or I won't be able to deal with everyone's issues tomorrow. These little green pills have become my life saver and will put me to sleep in a heartbeat. That's just what I need. I must go to sleep, because then I won't worry about where my husband is and won't be aware of the quivers in my stomach.

Ring, buzz, ring, buzz, goes the alarm clock. My head feels like I've been hit with a sledgehammer. I can't go to work; I won't be able to function. I slowly open my eyes and am surprised to see Ethan lying next to me. Wow, I didn't even hear him come in or feel him get in the bed, those little pills really work. I pounce on him! My fists are tagging his face and arms.

"Hey, hold up, what's wrong with you?"

"Don't even try it, where were you last night? I called you and you didn't bother to call me at all! I texted you! Ethan, where were you?"

"Babe, calm down."

"Don't tell me to calm down! You have some explaining to do and you better start now! I am so serious right now! Where were you?"

5

"My battery died. I didn't get any calls last night, slow down."

"Oh, you could have found a way to call me, text me, something! Did you even try to call to let me know what was going on? Where was your charger? You stayed out at least until 3 in the morning and you think I am supposed to be happy about that! The only thing you can say is your battery died! I'm so sick of this, I can't do this anymore! Where were you?"

I can't form words; I cry. I'm absolutely fed up with the lies and unexplained trips and charges on the credit card bill. He has an explanation for every suspicion that I have. He attended the school of liars and passed with honors. I feel him touch my shoulder; I jerk away.

"Don't touch me!"

"Susan, calm down, you are overreacting. I was out with the guys and just lost track of time. We got caught up in the game and started talking and before I knew it, it was late. I thought you were sleep. Babe, calm down, it is nothing going on, just having a good time with the boys. I'm sorry I didn't call, honestly, I thought you were sleep."

"Seriously Ethan, you said you would be right back and that was at 8. You said nothing about watching the game! You said nothing about an errand! You could have called. If you don't want to be married, just tell me right now. This is insane!"

"Wait, don't start that again. I'm not going anywhere," he lifts my chin and gently wipes the tears off my cheeks.

"I have told you a million times, if this isn't what you want just let me know and I'll give you a divorce."

"Susan, I love you. Call in today and we can spend some time together. Just you and me, baby girl, you know I love you," he coos with a smile.

I pick up the phone and inform my office manager that I am not feeling well and will forward the calls to voice mail.

"I 'm not staying off for us to spend time together. I need some time to think, to clear my head. I need to figure all of this out, it's just too much."

He looks at me, "Well, can I have a little sugar before I leave?"

I just stare at him, "You've got to be joking right," I reply in disbelief.

"Well, I'll be in the shower in case you change your mind, join me if you want this."

"You can't be serious, I hate you!" I scream.

I call my best friend, Tina. I need someone to listen and to convince me that I'm right, she's a voice of reason.

"Hello," Tina answers in a scratchy morning voice.

"Hey T, what's up?"

"Susan, why are you calling so early? It's not even 7o'clock yet, is everything alright?"

"Well, yeah, but I'm not going to work today. Are you off today? I thought maybe we could have breakfast or something."

"Oh no, what trick did Ethan pull now? I know that's it. Did he come home late?" she asks with disgust intertwined in her voice.

"He's still here, so I can't talk."

She sighs, "I'm off today. Come over and I'll cook breakfast. Bring some juice because I don't think there's any left."

"Alright, see you in a few."

Tina and I have been best friends since seventh grade. We have gone through everything together. She is the one person that I can always depend on; she has my back even if I'm wrong. Tina is bold and has no filter. Whatever she wants to say, she does. Whatever she wants, she goes after it, until it has her name written all over it. It is Tina's way or no way. I never worry about anything when she's around. If I come up short, she takes up the slack. Tina can finish my sentences before I even know what I want to say. That girl is my rock.

Ethan doesn't like her and calls her a busy body. They've had some heated arguments and I am always right in the middle to play referee. He thinks that I talk to her more than I talk to him. Of course, that is not true and he is exaggerating. The real reason he can't stand her is because she will always tell me I deserve better. She even said it in front of him a couple of times. She jokes that she has a divorce attorney on retainer for me, and knowing Tina, she probably does.

I know that Ethan is a good man. However, recently he is so distracted and distant. We hardly spend any time together and when we do, I end up getting so frustrated with him about the smallest things. We usually end up arguing and then he leaves. Honestly, it's not about unloading the dishwasher or leaving wet towels on the bathroom floor. The truth is simple; my husband is pulling away from me and I don't know why. There is a problem, but how can I fix something that I am not even sure I want anymore. Maybe, my life will be better without the strain of Ethan. Just like Tina said, save your energy to fight for something you want to keep. Right now, I don't know what I want. Is my marriage worth fighting for?

"So, what are you going to do today?" he asks as he dries his back.

I'm silent. He hates it when I ignore him. Though I'm mad at him, he looks good standing in front of the mirror. His body was the first thing that attracted me to him. His complexion is unbelievably smooth and his mocha skin tone compliments his soul burning eyes. It has been at least a month since we made love and it is getting harder for me to resist his advances. I don't want to make love to him because I have a sick feeling that he is having sex with someone else. The thought of it makes me want to puke.

"Hey baby girl, this is your last chance, are we making love?"

I glare at him, then look away.

"You need to get it together. It's been a long time. Tonight, you better be ready. I am making love to my wife," he announces as he kisses me on the neck.

"Whatever," I reply.

If I tell the truth, I want him to jump in bed with me and make love to me, right now. I turn from him and pick out something to wear from the closet, then head to the bathroom. He kisses me again before I close the bathroom door. The hot water awakens every nerve ending in my body.

The sluggishness slowly releases me from its clutches. I start to reflect, and deep down inside I want my marriage to work more than anything. Ethan and I dated for two years before getting married. He was so attentive and made me feel like I was the only woman on earth. He would surprise me with flowers and dates to art galleries. Ethan loves to write and he puts words on paper that put visions of him in my mind all day and night. Our relationship is built on loving each other and being each other's strength. It's about helping me face my fears and conquering them so that my dreams can be given birth and multiply. Not anymore, I feel abandoned, mad and confused!

It shouldn't be a surprise that I have become the best detective in the world, seeking out any information that will confirm the mind twisting agony that he is cheating on me. Then again, maybe my detective skills aren't that fantastic, because I have failed to discover that one crucial link. You know, that one piece of gotcha information that he can't explain away. I'm not going to think about this anymore. I am having a spoil Susan day, forget Ethan, at least for now.

I make it to Tina's house around 8:30. The fragrance of grits, fried chicken and biscuits is the perfect morning greeter.

"T, I can't believe you made all of this, it smells so good."

"You're the one that called so early and because I couldn't go back to sleep, I just got up and cooked."

"Trust, I'm not complaining."

We fix our plates and start to eat. Tina has been cooking since middle school. She was responsible for cooking the meals for her family when her mom had to work double shifts at the hospital. Now, she is a nurse and usually works double shifts herself. Tina never complains because she loves the money and always vows never to get married or have kids because they are too constricting. She loves pencil freedom, you know, pencil freedom. It means the freedom to change whenever and whatever you want, just erase people and things out of your life.

"Alright, spill it, what did Mr. Ethan Donovan do now?" she asks rolling her eyes and dramatically shaking her head.

"He didn't come home until after 3 last night. Sister girl, I called him like a thousand times and he never called back. He claims that the battery died on the phone and that he didn't have a charger."

She takes a bite of her chicken, "Do you believe that? Please tell me you don't, please tell me, you can't be that stupid. Sweetness, that's straight drama! You know, he could have charged that phone."

"I don't believe him, but I don't have any proof either that he isn't telling the truth. I want to believe him, but then again, I know he is lying. It's making me sick. I feel nauseated all day and can't even sleep. I'm a mess. This stress has my cycle late to, hmm."

"When is the last time you had sex?"

"About four weeks ago," I answer, smearing plum jelly on my biscuit.

"For real, no one's husband is going without sex for that long, not unless he is dying, his wife had a baby, or he ran out of his little blue pills. And in all those cases, he would still be trying to get some.

9

Has he tried to get some?" she asks staring at me.

I feel like her hazel eyes are penetrating my soul's core.

"Well kind of, he says little stuff," I feel uneasy.

"Has he thrown you on the bed and started kissing you or sneaking a peek while you're in the shower? Has he tried to sneak some when you are sleeping?" Tina rattles off the questions like I was in an interrogation room.

Now I'm embarrassed, "No", I say as I look down into my glass of grapefruit juice avoiding her glare.

"I think you have all the proof you need. He is hitting it off with someone else. C'mon girl wake up. Ethan is dogging you out. You don't have to take this mess. You need some time to think and separate yourself from the situation. I know a good divorce attorney. Now is the time to load your bullets for the fight, divorce him! You don't need him. I'm your friend, you deserve better. Hang him out to dry and keep it moving on down the train track!"

Tears roll down my face and I can't look at Tina right now because she has confirmed what I knew. The two of us sit in ear shattering silence. She reaches across the table and hold my hand. I sit there for a little longer. Tina strokes the back of my hand.

"You know what you need to do, handle it," Tina states in a gentle whisper.
I wipe my face with a paper towel and take several mind clearing deep breaths. I feel a transition in my spirit. I close my eyes and let the silence penetrate every crevice of my brain. I take my hand out of Tina's. I grab my purse; I feel renewed.

"Susan, where are you going?" Tina asks with a baffled look.

"I've got to save my marriage. I need to fight for my husband! What am I thinking? He belongs to me and I belong to him. I'll call you later and let you know what happens, thanks for breakfast."

"What," Tina is confused. "Wait, you're making a mistake!"

I spend the entire afternoon getting ready for the first step in winning back Ethan. Even though I don't know who I am competing with, I am going to give her a run for her money. She can't have something that belongs to me. I stood at the altar and made vows to God and to Ethan. My husband did not make any vows to her. He is my husband! I am not having a poor mouth party anymore; it is time to take action. At the mall I buy a sexy nightie, a white halter top trimmed in cotton candy pink fur and a matching G-string. My hair stylist cuts my hair into a layered Bob, yep, it is too cute. My next stop is the grocery store. I pick out two perfectly trimmed Filet Mignon steaks, strawberries, grapes, candles, a bouquet of pink and white tulips, and a bag of salad mix. Tonight, will be perfect. By the time I get home it is a little after 5o'clock. I called Ethan earlier and told him that he needed to be home by 6:00. I had just enough time to get everything ready. I am sexy hot and ready to seduce my husband!

"Bam, I look good," I exclaim as I admire myself in the mirror. I turn around to check out my booty. Umm, we may have to eat dinner later and handle our love business first. I am tremendously excited about seeing his reaction and the big surprise that I need to share with him. Whoa, I was really surprised, wait until he sees this!

I run a hot bath for him and put his new white silk boxers on the bed. All the lights in the condo are off and the candles create a seductive golden glow throughout the rooms. My stomach does a flip just thinking about his reaction when he opens the door. Finally, 6:00 comes, the lock clicks and the doorknob turn. I stand in front of the door and Ethan's eyes widens. He grins and rubs his hands together.

"If you are up for the challenge, drop your clothes and surrender now. I am ready for you. What's up?"

"You are definitely in charge. Just tell me what you want me to do," he says as he quickly takes off his clothes, "I surrender all!"

I lead him to the bathroom where I give him a bath and feed him grapes and strawberries. The lavender bath gel and vanilla candles intertwine and scents the bathroom. He is hypnotized. I smile as he slips on the boxers.

"Whoa, these are a little cold."

"I promise you will be very hot in a minute," I remark as I kiss his neck and slowly make my way to his inviting mouth. He kisses me so passionately I almost lose my cool. It seems as though I am kissing him for the first time. Our tongues explore each other's mouth, as if getting reacquainted. It is fabulous; I love my husband!

We quickly eat dinner; I don't remember even tasting the flavor of the food. I could have served dirt and we both would have thought it was a delicacy. Ethan sweeps me up in his arms and gently places me on our bed. We kiss for what seems like hours. I allow my mind and body to be loved by him, my husband.

11

"Susan, I love you," he whispers between kisses.

"Do you really love me, Ethan? Don't say it if it's not true."

"I want this marriage more than anything in the world. I will prove that to you for the rest of my life," he declares as he slips off my halter top. He is being so gentle with me.

I'm so happy to hear those words. I can't hold back the tears. He gently wipes them away and kisses my eyelids. The drought is over. I swear I am taken to another planet. Ethan hadn't made love to me like that in months. My mind, soul and body feel like I have been dipped in molten lava and then doused with water from an arctic iceberg, he is absolutely incredible. His reaction tells me I am just as incredible.

"Ethan, I love you."

I am about to get up and give him his surprise, but he pulls me back into his embrace.

"I have something for you, a big surprise. I need to get it now," I whisper.

"Trust me it can wait," he says kissing my ear. I close my eyes and snuggle into his arms. I have won the first battle. We are going to make it, I feel it. This feels like the first time and I am happy.

I sit up startled by the ringing of the phone. I lay back down waiting for Ethan to pick it up, but it continues to ring.

"Hello"

"Hello, I'm calling to offer you a deal on a prescription drug plan."

I immediately hang up and press block on the phone.

I am listening for the sound of the television in the living room. The condo is eerily quiet. I had fallen asleep and didn't even know it. How long have I been asleep? I can't believe him. Where is Ethan and what time is it?

I call out, "Ethan! Hey, where are you shugga?"

Nothing, where is he? I look on the dresser and there is a note that simply states, I'll be back. How long has he been gone? Did he just leave? I look at the clock, 10:43. Wow, I've been sleep for a few hours. I grab the phone and call him. I wait 10 minutes and call again, straight to voice mail. I text. I search his feed to see if he posted anything, nothing. I can't believe this is happening, after the incredible time we just had. What was so important that he had to leave? Why

12

didn't he wake me up? I feel my chest tightening with anger and disbelief. I rest my head on the pillow and try to calm down, it's not working. I need a sleeping pill. No, I can't take those anymore. I need Tina. I dial her number, no answer. I remember that she's on call; she's probably at the hospital. I decide to watch television until he comes home.

It's 11:36, I've waited long enough. Tina is right; I need time to get myself together. He's going to get a taste of his own medicine. I quickly put on jeans and a t- shirt. I throw a couple of outfits in an overnight bag. Thankfully, it's Friday. I will get a room for the weekend and decide on my next move. I open my purse to grab the car keys. There it is, the golden box with the iridescent bow, my big surprise. I untie the bow and slowly lift the lid off of the box. There are two lines, one in the test window and one in the result window. I rub my hand across my stomach and imagine Ethan's reaction to my big surprise; we are going to have a baby. Though we didn't plan the pregnancy I think it might get us on track. Several months ago, we talked about starting to plan for a baby, but now what will happen? Am I going to be a single mom? Can a baby get Ethan's mind off the other woman? Questions are scattered all over my mind.

I want to go somewhere out of the way, just in case he tries to look for me. I don't want to be found. I drive in silence, except for the question of why drumming on my brain. After driving a couple of hours, I decide to stop at the next motel. I am exhausted.

"Good evening, may I help you?" the man asks.

"Yes sir, I would like one of your suites for the weekend."

I hand him my credit card and license. He stares at me as he waits for the computer to print the receipt. I'm sure I look a mess and he probably can tell I've been crying.

"Just sign here and here is your license and credit card; enjoy your stay at Rest Easy Inn and Suites. We have a complimentary buffet breakfast in the morning from 7 to 10 in the lobby."

I take the key card and look at the number, 430. I don't want to think about anyone or anything. I step inside the elevator and press 4 on the number panel; the door shuts. This must be the slowest elevator in the world. I should have taken the stairs. The elevator stops, but the door doesn't open. I look up and the number 3 is lit. I press 4 again, still the elevator is lifeless. Please don't tell me I'm gonna get trapped in an elevator. Then the doors open, there is a couple standing in the hall. They don't notice me because they are locked in a deep kiss. Then it happens. I recognize the back of Tina's head. Yes, it's Tina. I wait for her to stop kissing this guy so I can see his face. I press the button, to stop the elevator doors from closing. Tina turns around.

I wave at her. Her eyes widen as she stands frozen in front of me. I eagerly wait for her man to step around her. I continue to press the open-door button on the elevator. I'm about to step off the elevator to talk to her. In an instant, he pulls her around to face him again, my breathing stops. I catch a glimpse of him; it's Ethan! Tina pulls away from him to face me. They both stand staring at me. The three of us don't say anything, stillness, the three of us stunned in a moment.

I shut my eyes and try to grab my breath. I hear the primal scream building in my soul. The rage grows more potent with each second, until it controls every cell in my body.

"Susan, um, wait a minute, hold up Susan," Ethan stammers.

I let out an explosive yell and tackle Tina to the floor because she is standing directly in front of me. I straddle her; my hands grip her neck until my knuckles burn. My fingernails dig into her soft flesh and the warmth and stickiness of her blood covers my fingers. Tina is desperately trying to shove me off her; she tries to grab my hands. She can't! I feel her nails scratching at my face. I pound her head against the floor, slamming her head up and down and up and down, screaming with each slam. Time stands still and I only hear the slight drumming of my heart and a heaving sound coming from somewhere in the nooks of my soul.

Ethan and another man pull me off Tina. She is on the floor writhing, coughing and holding her neck. Ethan holds me. I pull free of him and lunge for his face and kick him in the groin. Suddenly, I am violently thrown to the floor by two security guards; my face is pressed on the carpet. I feel their knees on my back, pinning me to the floor. I sob. They lift me up and shove me in the elevator, then I am escorted to an office. The room is spinning and I feel like I'm floating. A man walks in and stands in front of me.

"What is going on? I need an explanation right now," he demands.

I try to answer. I think I am speaking, but I don't hear any words. I stare at the wall. Someone is knocking. It's one of the security guards. They talk in hushed tones and then they both leave the room. I am alone. I am drained. I struggle to find evidence that I'm alive and that this is happening. Pull yourself together, I mumble over and over. It doesn't help. The heaving won't stop; the pounding in my head won't stop; the stabbing in my heart won't stop; the waterfall of tears won't stop!

I think I hear Ethan's voice. Yes, he is in the hallway. He pleads with them not to call the police and to let him handle it. I focus on trying to get myself together. I'm trying to stop crying. I need to splash water on my face and wash the blood off my hands. I can't regulate my breathing; I'm gasping for air.

There's a restroom inside the office where I am. I walk inside and close the door. I try to stop the hysterical wailing that is coming from the valley of my heart. I look in the mirror and don't recognize myself. Black streaks of mascara etch a pattern on my face. One golden hoop earring dangles in my ear. The other one is gone. The diamond pendant necklace is no longer around my neck and my shirt is ripped. My purple bra is barely hidden. There's a long scratch under my left eye and a knot on my forehead.

Suddenly, I feel an excruciating pain in my stomach. It's the only pain that I am aware of; it hits me again. I double over as the pain drags me to the floor. Something warm gushes out from between my legs, blood runs down my legs. I bellow as my body expels the savior of my marriage. Oh God, I am losing our child! I scream for help. I reach up from the floor and grab the doorknob. I push the door open and scream louder.

"Please call an ambulance, I need help, somebody help me!"

"I have someone getting help for you, I'm Sharon, the manager," she reaches for my hand and kneels next to me.

"I'm so scared, what is happening, I'm scared. Help me, please," I beg in between sobs and screams.

"Shh, stop crying, is your name Susan?"

Crying hysterically, I answer, "Yes, I'm Susan, I need help!"

I plead with her not to leave me. I tell her I'm having a miscarriage. I continue to sob and my body is shaking.

"Close your eyes and I'm going to pray for you. You are going to be alright. Everything is going to be fine. Susan, let's pray."

I close my eyes and tighten the grip on her hand. A sharp pain rips through my stomach, more blood gushes out of me.

"Lord, I ask you to let Susan feel your peace right now. Surround her in your love and calm her down. Let her know that You are able to take care all situations if she will trust you. Jesus, we need You right now, shift this atmosphere, Lord, touch her mind and body and bring peace that surpasses all understanding as only You can. Lord, I love you and thank you for answering my prayer, Amen."

I don't feel scared.

"Thank you for helping me. I appreciate you."

"You are welcome and thank God," she replies as she helps me off the floor. Despite what I have lost I feel like I have gained something. I hear sirens, but I am not fearful, instead there is a calmness that envelopes me. I've never experienced this peace before. I look at Sharon. I don't know her, but there is something about her that makes me want to know her. There is kindness in her voice.

"Did they call the police?" I quietly ask.

"No, we talked to Mr. Donovan and the other guest, and both of them insisted that we did not need to, but we did call an ambulance for you. I'm going to step out so that the paramedics can come in here. Susan, I'll be right outside the door. You are going to be okay."

Ethan is standing by the door when she opens it. He rushes inside the restroom. We look at each other. The paramedics hurry to my side.

"Sir, please step out of the way," the paramedic instructs.

"She's my wife. I need to know what happened to her. I need to make sure she is alright. Susan, tell him I can stay with you, please, baby? I can't leave. I need to be with you. I am so sorry. I am!"

Ethan's face is twisted with uncertainty and agony. He looks vulnerable and frightened. I don't say anything.

"Sir, step outside," the paramedic says a bit firmer.

'Susan, I am right here. I'm not going anywhere. I will be right outside this door. I'm sorry and I love you. We gotta talk! I am sorry!"

I don't say anything to him. I just nod. Despite all that has happened, calmness was hugging me.

"Mya"

I tug at my shirt and try to make sure my butt is covered. I run my fingers through my hair and pull it more around my chin; I purposely roller set my hair, in order for it to be curly. When my hair is curly, it hides more of my face. I suck in my stomach and open the door. The living room is filled with white and pink balloons. I smile as I place my hand over the back of the couch, which is still partially covered in the delivery plastic. Momma insists that the plastic will help the furniture stay new and is needed just in case someone spills something on it; that was seven years ago. I'm greeted with the smell of peach cobbler. There is no denying the smell of my favorite food. I hear the shrill laughter of my sisters coming from the family room. My stomach starts to knot up and I immediately wish I was home.

"Mya, how long have you been in here?" my sister Paula asks as she passes the living room on her way to the bathroom.

"I just walked in," I reply sucking in my stomach.

"Momma, Mya here!" Paula yells.

I walk in the family room and flash a sunshine smile.

"Hey Momma's baby girl!" my mother exclaims.

"Happy Birthday!" I shout as I hug her.

Just then Paula enters the room; she walks over and hugs me.

I suck in my stomach and hug her as quickly as possible. She pinches my cheeks and my side.

"I'm glad you lost few pounds," she announces as she walks around me looking me up and down.

I feel like a slave on the auction block being reviewed by a potential master.

"No, no Paula, please I am pleading, just leave her alone," Momma demands.

My other sisters, Marian and Traci, look at me and smile. I hug them and quickly sit down. I feel like I'm going to pass out. I have on a full body slimmer, a girdle and control top pantyhose. I take quick small breaths because I don't want to exhale too much and make my stomach bulge out even more.

Marian sips tea and Traci walks into the kitchen with Momma.

"Mya, how have you been doing?" asks Marian.

"Great and how are my two beautiful nieces?"

17

"They are just fine and they want to know when their Auntie Mya is going to come get them for the weekend. Baby girl, I hope it's soon," Marian remarks playfully.

"Tell them to give me a call and we will set a date."

I moved about one hundred miles away from home because I need my space and our family can be draining.

Momma comes back in and sits next to me on the couch.

"So, what is going on with my baby girl?" Momma asks.

Before I have time to answer, Paula answers for me.

"Cooking and eating is what it looks like to me," replies Paula as she shakes her head to show her disapproval.

Traci rolls her eyes at Paula and then looks at me.

"Mya, I know you aren't going to let her get away with that," Traci says standing in front of me.

"I'm not listening to her," I remark and flip my hand to show I am not concerned.

"Please don't start today," Momma pleads, "it's my 70th birthday and I want to enjoy it with my girls. I wish your father could be here, bless his soul. I miss him so much, my sweet husband."

"Paula, come help me set the table," Marian suggests as she sits her tea down on the counter.

The food smells wonderful, suddenly my stomach growls really loud. I clear my throat to try to distract from it.

"Oh Momma, I forgot your gift in the car. I'll be right back."

I need to prepare myself for dinner. I left the gift in the car on purpose, just in case I needed to get away for a few minutes.

I reach in the back seat and grab the purple gift bag and a pack of saltine crackers. I stuff two crackers in my mouth, and then gulp down some water. I eat two more crackers and drank the remaining water. Saltine crackers and water has been my breakfast, lunch and dinner for the last two weeks. I was trying desperately to lose a few pounds before Momma's party. I am so hungry.

"Mya, come on," Momma yells from the porch.

I brush the crumbs from around my mouth and close the car door. Alrighty, here goes nothing, whew.

"Baby girl, don't let Paula get to you," she whispers as she kisses my cheek. I smile and walk into the dining room. There are large colorful ceramic bowls on the table filled with golden pork chops, corn on the cob, string beans with pearl onions, saffron rice, and butter-soaked cornbread muffins. I sit at the table. Paula has already started to fill the plates with food. She's very generous with the portions. I'm next, I pass the plate.

"Mya, I know that you are on a diet, right?" she asks as she holds my empty plate in her hands.

"Kind of," I look down at the table to avoid her stare.

"I knew I was right. I made something just for you!" she exclaims as she trots off to the kitchen.

When she brings my plate back there is a single scoop of cottage cheese in the center of the plate, a slice of apple on each side and ten carrot sticks. She places the plate in front of me; my eyes fill with tears. I rapidly blink to make the tears go away.

"You know what, you have got some nerves," Traci declares shaking her head in disbelief and picking up my plate.

"You doing too much," Marian says looking at Paula.

"I'm looking out for my sister. What do you think I'm doing? Do you want her to die early? Well, that is what is going to happen if everyone keeps on pretending that she isn't fat. She is too fat and too much weight is not healthy. She has a cute face, but she is too big!" Paula asserts as she sits at the table. The whole room shifts.

"Who made you Mya's wellness coach?" Traci inquires as she dumps the food from my plate into the garbage can. She walks back to the table and piles food on my plate from the colorful bowls. Paula stands and places her hands on her hips. She pushes in her chair, almost knocking it over. She stomps over to where I'm sitting and stands next to me. I'm anxious. Ugh, I knew this was going to happen.

"Mya, how tall are you?" Paula vehemently asks.

"About 5'5," I answer staring straight ahead.

Paula looks at Traci. Traci places the plate in front of me. Traci stands on the other side of me and locks her eyes on Paula. Grains of rice fall on the table from the mound of rice that Traci has piled on my plate. I'm stuck in the middle of my warring sisters. Both of them are ready to make their point and snatch each other's head off in the process. It's a standoff and I want to disappear!

"Traci, do you honestly think that someone her height can carry all of this weight?" she places her hand on my shoulder, "She probably weighs a good 220. Maybe, even more than that!"

19

"180," I whisper, "Paula, I weigh 180, maybe 181."

"It is none of your business how much she weighs!" Traci yells as she slams two muffins on my plate. One of them splits in half.

"The two of you sit down before you ruin my day," Momma requests looking at Traci and then at Paula. Momma is uncomfortable.

Marian glances up at us and continues to eat. She shakes more hot sauce on her pork chop and bites into it. Traci and Paula sit down. I pick up a fork and start to eat. I chew slowly and keep my eyes on the plate. We eat in silence. I feel bad for Momma; I ruined her day.

"Baby girl, how did everything taste? I hope you left room for peach cobbler," Momma says nodding, as if to let me know it's ok for me to have it.

Traci looks at Paula anticipating a response, but she doesn't say anything. I really want that cobbler, but I am scared.

"Momma, make my cobbler to go. I'm working the late shift tonight," Marian says leaving the table.

"I will do that and give you some extra to take to my grandbabies. Let them know Nana sends it with lots of love!"

"Mya, do you want something else?" Traci asks eyeballing Paula. She is getting ready for the next round of the battle.

"I hope not," Paula replies biting into her corn and staring back at Traci. They are both set and ready to make their point.

"Actually, I'm quite full," I reply, looking to call a truce.

Paula reaches for another pork chop and then stops.

"You don't need this piece. I'll take it," Paula declares as she removes the pork chop from my plate. Bam, here we go.

Traci reaches across the table and snatches it out of Paula's hand and slams it back on my plate. A few crumbs fall in my lap.

"Traci, don't even start with me. She ate half of a pork chop, corn and almost all of her rice. Now Momma is giving her cobbler. I'm trying to help her. You need to stop it and face reality. All of us are physically fit, except Mya. She is cursed with Daddy's family fat tendency. Thank God we took after Momma, but she didn't and she needs to work harder than the rest of us. I'm 5'7, you are 5'8 and Marian is, what, 5'7 and a half. Mya is only 5'4 and can't carry all of that weight. Just look at her! Keep pretending she ain't a big girl and she will be a fat dead girl! All of you need to face reality, she fat!"

"Paula, shut up, just stop talking! I can't believe you! Mya is grown and her weight is not your business. You are rude and!"

Paula doesn't let Traci finish.

"No man wants to marry a big girl. She has a beautiful face, but she is overweight. She is 28 and weighs a ton, hell maybe even two tons! I am looking out for my sister because I love her."

Paula walks over to me and cups my face in her hands as she kisses my forehead.

"Mya, I only want what is best for you," she says kissing my forehead again, then tenderly brushing her cheek against mine.

"Mya, tell her to get out of your face and to stop giving you unsolicited advice. Paula sit down and leave her alone! You can lose a few pounds yourself!" Traci yells as she stands ready to protect me.

Momma walks in the dining room carrying a tray with bowls of peach cobbler with scoops of vanilla ice cream.

"What did I miss? What are you two arguing about? Hush up both of you. Everyone come in the family room so I can open my gifts, let's have peace. I mean it, stop all of this, right now."

"Did Marian leave?" Paula asks somewhat puzzled.

"Yes, Paula," Momma responds.

"She never visits for long," Paula says rolling her eyes.

"I wonder why," Traci answers, looking at Paula.

Momma sits on the couch next to me and starts to take the tissue paper out of the gift bag.

"Baby girl this gown is darling, thank you very much."

Momma opens her other presents and we sit around looking at photo albums. For a little while, the attention is off me and I'm glad.

"Momma I better be going," I announce.

"Alright baby girl, call me as soon as you get home."

"Call me tonight," Traci says with a wink.

"I will and thank you, I love you sis."

Before I walk out the door Momma places a covered plate in my hand and puts an aluminum foil covered bowl on top of it.

"You can have this for dinner tomorrow. Maybe you can eat it in peace. Mya, you are my beautiful baby girl."

"Thank you, Momma, I love you and Happy Birthday."

I open the car door and get inside. I place the plate and bowl on the passenger's seat. I am about to drive away, but Paula runs to the door. Really, what could she possibly have to say to me.

"Mya, wait," she yells throwing her arms up in the air.

She walks around on the passenger's side and I unlock the door. She picks the plate and bowl up off the seat, she sits down, then places the plate and bowl in her lap.

"I just want to say that I love you and care for you, for real."

I nod, but I don't say anything. As she gets out of the car, the plate and bowl slip from her hands and hits the pavement with a thump.

"Oh no, sorry," Paula says bending to pick up the mess.

"Don't worry about it," I lean over and close the door. I spin off. I look in the rearview mirror and watch Paula walk toward the house. I drive a few blocks and pull into the parking lot of the Burger Palace. I quickly walk to the restroom and pull off the pantyhose, the girdle and the body slimmer. I run my hand across the deep groove that encircles my waist, which has been created by the tight elastic. I look in the mirror and pull my hair back behind my ears and stare at myself. Paula is right. I'm too young to be fat. I open the restroom door and the smell of french fries hits my nose. Hypnotically, I walk up to the counter and order a jumbo order of fries and an extra-large mocha cherry shake. I open the bag and stuff the hot fries in my mouth. I chew them quickly and warmth fills my mouth. The salt makes my taste buds twirl with delight. I take a long sip of the shake. The cold ice cream coats my throat. It's the perfect mix of rich chocolate and sweet cherries. I savor the chocolate cherry sweetness. The shake tickles the back of my throat and I enjoy every moment. I love food, the taste of it, the smell of it and the different textures.

I am happy to be back in my safe place, my apartment. I walk straight to the fridge. There is only a pack of saltines, half a lemon, and a gallon of water. Every time I have an upcoming visit with my Momma and sisters, I deprive myself of food. I don't want to look too fat, so that Paula won't get started with her advice. Dang, I'm still hungry! I pick up the phone and call Pizza and Thangs.

"Hello P and T, may I take your order?"

"Hi, what are your specials?"

"We have the super family meal deal for $15.99."

"What comes with that?"

"You get a large one topping pizza, 10 wings, an order of butter cheese bread sticks and an orange 2-liter soda."

"I'll take that and two fudge brownie squares."

I give him the delivery information and feel joyful that my food is on the way. I change into my pajamas and turn on the television. There isn't anything fascinating on television. There was some show on about common household poisons and how kids are injured yearly from swallowing toxic substances in the home. Then I see the answer to my weight problem. Whoa, ipecac syrup. It's a liquid that induces vomiting. I had tried vomiting after my meals before, but I could never get with sticking a toothbrush down my throat or even my finger. Gag with a finger, no thanks. Instead, after every meal if I take a little of this it would make me vomit. I wasn't going to starve myself. Nope, I'm a big girl that loves her food. I think I can do this long enough to lose a few pounds and then everyone will be happy. I'm excited about my new discovery! By doing this I don't have to give up tasting my food or even eating it. I can eat as much as I want and delight in the taste and then just get rid of it.

Dang it, I forgot to call Momma.

"Hello"

"Hi, Momma"

"I'm glad you made it in baby girl. Did everything go well?"

"Yes, traffic wasn't bad at all. I'm about to go to bed."

"Wait, Traci wants to talk to you, hang on for a second."

"Hey Mya"

"Hi, thanks for all you did for me today."

"Listen, you don't need to thank me. I 'm just so sick of Paula being so rude and thinking she can say anything she wants to you. Mya, you don't have to take that crap from her. She does it, because she knows that you won't say anything. You need to check her."

"But maybe, she is right. I am too fat. It wouldn't hurt for me to drop a few pounds. For real I want to lose a few pounds."

"When you are ready to start dieting let me know and I will help you any way that I can. But, don't do it for Paula or anyone else. Do it for you. Do you hear me? Do it cause that's what you want to do, call me baby girl and we'll chat or text me tomorrow, okay."

"Thanks Traci and kiss Momma for me."

"I got you and love you, goodnight Mya."

The doorbell rings. I pay and open the pizza box. The room suddenly fills with the aroma of garlic and tomatoes. I pick up two slices and fold them together and take a big bite. The cheese swings from my lip and I twirl my tongue around it to keep it from falling back into the box. My tongue separates the flavors, the tangy tomato sauce, the buttery crust, the fresh garlic, oregano, and the salty beef topping. I chew with my eyes closed and concentrate on the feel of the cheese in my mouth and the infusion of all of the flavors. I open the orange soda and drink it right from the bottle. Next, I eat the wings. The sweet and sour sauce is a good contrast to the pizza. Within an hour, I have finished the entire meal except for the soda. I change into a sweat suit and grab my purse. I drive to the drug store and to talk to the pharmacist.

"Hi, how can I help you?"

"I'm looking for ipecac syrup."

"It is on aisle three. Do you have kids at home?"

"It is for the kids that I baby sit. A good sitter is always prepared," I respond with a smile.

"Make sure that you call the poison control center before you administer the syrup. When a child swallows some poisons, you should not induce vomiting, because it can cause more damage. Also, make sure that you read the label for correct use and interactions."

I interrupt her, "Thank you, but I'm not a teen babysitter. I know what I'm doing," I reply with a little annoyance in my voice.

"No problem, I'm just making sure you understand."

As soon as I get home, I open it and take a tablespoon full. Yuck, I don't enjoy that taste at all. I sit on the bathroom floor next to the toilet. Wow, the smell of the spring mountain toilet bowl freshener is overpowering, as I sit resting my elbows on the toilet's rim. I wait nervously to see the results. After a few minutes, I gag. I can't control it. I get up on my knees and reposition myself over the toilet just in time. A large amount of vomit hurls from my mouth and plops into the toilet. It's so forceful that some of it splatters on the floor and down the front of my sweatshirt. Huge chunks fly out of my mouth and I gasp for air. I flush the toilet and stand. I'm nervous and my mouth tastes like I have been sucking on pennies. I rinse my mouth with cool water and look in the mirror. I smile, not too bad, although my throat stings a little. I shower, brush my teeth and get in the bed.

The next morning, I put the brown bottle in my cosmetic pouch, inside of my purse. I never want to leave home without it. I

24

can always take a sip after lunch and throw up without anyone knowing. Yes, I have all the privacy that I need. I love my job because I'm not always stuck in an office. I'm a city inspector. I make visits to various neighborhoods to make sure the homes and businesses are following city ordinance compliance laws and codes. I feel hopeful about my new plan.

It's about 11:30 and I'm starving. I pull into the Chicken Pit Stop and order lunch. I drive to a park around the block, and park under a huge Oak tree to savor my meal. I devour the four-piece chicken dinner with sides of mashed potatoes and fried okra. The chicken isn't as good as Momma's or mine, but decent. I shake the syrup and take a sip. I swing open the car door and wait for the vomit to rush to my mouth. It does and I throw up right there in the parking lot. I take out a bottle of mouthwash, swirl it around my mouth and spit it out on top of the vomit pile. I'm ready to go!

Over the next couple of months my routine becomes flawless, eat, vomit, and brush. I see results. At first, I only vomited after lunch and dinner. However, now anytime I eat something I throw it up afterwards. Doing it this way, I don't miss out on the taste and texture of my food. I even start taking vitamin supplements to make sure my body is getting the proper nutrients.

Then it happens, people start asking if I am losing weight, they say that they can tell. Hold me down baby, because I am about to float to the sky! Awe struck, no one has ever given me compliments like this before. Over the next three months I drop 32 pounds. I have to go home and show Ms. Paula that I have it all together. I decide to give Momma a surprise visit. Bam, how you like me now!

I'm so excited about my new look. I even pull my hair back into a ponytail and only wear one girdle this time. I arrive at Momma's house. Just as I am driving up, I notice Momma and Traci sitting on the porch. I blow the horn, to announce my arrival.

"Well, look at this, my baby girl is here!" Momma shouts as she stands up to greet me. She is beaming with a huge smile.

"Hi, Momma!" I say with pure happiness as I hug her.

"Mya, you've lost so much weight," Momma says looking at me. I can't quite tell is she is asking me or telling me.

"Yes, I have Momma," I exclaim as I playfully shake my hips.

"Are you alright, Mya? You have dark circles under your eyes and you look tired," Momma says with a look of concern on her face. Her mouth twists in unbelief; she just looks at me as if something is not quite right. I am not that happy about her reaction.

"I'm great!" I exclaim as I walk with an exaggerated bounce

"Hey Mya," Traci says kissing me on the cheek. "Baby girl look at you. Yes, Momma she has lost quite a bit of weight."

"Yep, look at me," I respond playfully, putting my hands on my hips. I am shaking my hips and walking in a circle.

Then the door opens and Paula steps outside. I wasn't expecting to see her because her car wasn't in the driveway.

"Oh my, I know this can't be Mya, my long lost sister that never visits, calls or text. Wait a minute! You've lost weight! I mean you are still fat, but not as fat as you were. How much weight have you lost?" Paula yells jumping up and down clapping her hands like she had just won the lottery. She is yelling and whooping.

"Almost forty pounds!" I exclaim and I start jumping like her.

"Great, wonderful, fabulous," Paula shouts still clapping her hands and laughing. We are in this weight loss happy dance together.

I have finally made Paula proud of me; I am content!

"Mya, do you want something to drink or eat?" Momma asks with a look of concern still entrenched in her brow.

"Momma, don't make Mya blow her diet. She is doing good and she doesn't need you filling her up with food. She still has about twenty or thirty pounds that she needs to lose. Let's not get too excited she is still fat, but making progress. Girl, you are doing it!"

"Paula, nope, don't start with that today. It is not that kind of day. If you don't shut up, then I won't take you to the mechanic to pick up your car. You need to worry about your man not paying the bills and him asking Momma if he can borrow two thousand dollars, worry about that Ms. Paula and not Mya," Traci snaps, as she waits for Paula to say something, so the battle can start.

Paula shoot dagger eyes at Traci and replies, "If you don't know what you are talking about then you should just keep your mouth shut! Stay out of my business, which is none of your business!"

Paula sits next to Momma and crosses her legs. She is ready for Traci to reply. But, she doesn't. We sit on the porch and talk about everything from the news to the neighbors. For the first time in a long time, I enjoy being around Paula. I would have never imagined that losing a few pounds could make a difference in how she treats me. Momma prepared club sandwiches and potato salad for lunch. It's delicious. Paula doesn't even comment on how much potato salad I put on my plate. Whew, such a relief. I can enjoy this day.

I get my purse and go in the bathroom. I sip the syrup and vomit, something's wrong. I vomit, but it's a mixture of bright red blood. I spit it out! I cough. The more I cough, the more blood rushes up my throat and flies out of my mouth. Something is wrong! I can't stop coughing! Chunks of food and blood splash in the toilet. I'm hyperventilating! I gasp for air. I can't get enough air in my lungs, whehe! huhehw! ohohoh! ughugh! more blood fills my mouth.

"Mya, are you ok?" Traci asks knocking on the door.
I can't answer because I can't stop coughing. I flush the toilet, but I need to spit the blood out again. My throat feels like someone is holding a blow torch to it! I'm sweating profusely and there is an intense pain in my chest. My vision is a little blurry.
"Mya, open the door, Mya, Mya, open the door!" Traci's voice sounds urgent. I don't want her to know what is happening, but I need her. I unlock the door. Traci rushes in and locks the door behind her.

"What is wrong? Why are you bleeding like this?"

I look up at her with tears in my eyes, "I don't know. I don't know, Traci."
She picks the bottle up off the sink and reads the label.

"Why are you taking this Mya? What is going on? What is this for? Did you just take some of this? Why? Wait, what is going on?"

I can't answer her because I'm vomiting again. This time it wasn't because of the syrup, it was nerves. Blood and bitter yellow slime fill my mouth. I spit it in the toilet and then flush it.

"I'm taking you to the hospital, come on," Traci demands pulling at my arm and helping me off the floor.

She stuffs the bottle in my purse and flushes the toilet again. She wipes my face with a washcloth and then sprays air freshener.

"Listen, we won't tell them where we are going. You just go get in the car and don't say anything. I'll handle Momma and Paula. You are going to be ok, I promise," Traci declares wiping my face again with a cold washcloth and kissing my forehead.

I walk out the bathroom and straight to the porch; I don't look at Momma or Paula. I head straight to Traci's car.

"Momma, we will be back I've got an important errand to run. I asked Mya to go with me," Traci says as she picks up her purse off the chair and quickly gets her keys.

"Where are you going? I hope you will be back to take me to get my car. Why didn't you ask me to go? I'll ride with you," Paula states standing to her feet.

"If I wanted you to go, I would have asked you. Obviously, I don't want you to go. I want Mya to go because she won't have my business all over the streets. So, sit right on back down."

"It must have something to do with a man," Paula snaps back.

"Yep, you got it and it has absolutely nothing to do with you." Traci drives off. I recline the seat and start crying.

"Mya, you can tell me anything. What's wrong? Why are you sick? Please tell me what happened, my sweet baby girl."

"I've been taking something to make me throw up after I eat."

"What? Why, never mind, I'm going to help you. You will be fine Mya. Just try to relax and we are almost to the hospital."

We arrive to the hospital and I fill out the paper work and we wait. The wait isn't long and the nurse takes my vitals and I explain to her what I have been doing. Soon the doctor comes in and examines me; Traci stands by the bed the entire time. He informs me that they need to conduct an endoscopy immediately, to determine the damage to my throat; they prep me. I am scared.

Afterwards, the surgeon walks in to talk to me and Traci.

"You are lucky. You have a Mallory-Weiss tear. Also, you are dehydrated, and your potassium is low from all of the vomiting. You were playing a very dangerous game that could have ended in death. The tear will heal and thankfully you didn't have severe damage to your esophagus. You will need to schedule a follow up visit with your primary physician. I have set up appointments with our eating disorder center and a nutritionist. Do you have any questions for me?"

"No," I answer looking straight ahead. I am so embarrassed.

"You will stay overnight for observation and we'll continue to give you some fluids. If everything works out, you can go home probably tomorrow afternoon."

"I can't stay overnight, can I just go home please," I announce shaking my head.

Traci interrupts, "Thank you doctor, she will be staying."

28

"Traci, I can't stay, what will I tell Momma and Paula."

"I'll take care of them and I will stay here with you tonight. We have got to get you through this."

"Thank you, I love you."

"You need to get some sleep and I'll call Momma and tell her that I have to drive my friend somewhere and we will be back tomorrow. Does Momma have an extra key to your car?"

"Yes"

"I'll tell her to drive Paula to the mechanic. I'll take care of everything, don't worry."

I look at Traci and nod my head. She walks out the room and I close my eyes. I can't believe that I am so desperate. I bury my face in the pillow and cry. Traci comes back to the room and sits on the bed. She sits in caring silence with me and waits until I stop crying.

"I know that you are mad at me and I'm sorry, really, I didn't want anyone to find out. I am not only fat, but stupid. What is wrong with me?"

"No more of that crazy talk. I love you and you are not stupid. If something happened to you, I wouldn't know what to do with myself. I never want to hear those words again. You are not stupid."

"Traci, I just didn't know what else to do. Paula is right. I am fat and no one will want to marry me and," Traci gently places her hand over my mouth and leans in close to me.

"Be quiet, remember what Momma and Daddy always told us. They said that we were beautifully and wonderfully made by our Creator. That is still true. You are still beautiful, regardless of what the scale says and regardless of what Paula thinks. I've told you before, God is able to handle all of our problems, but we mess up things when we make choices based on the ignorance of others. You need to make better food choices and stop allowing Paula and anyone else to tear you down. Never give anyone that much power over you. You are strong and beautiful; you'll bounce back. You made a bad choice, but you're not bad."

I nod and she removes her hand from over my mouth.

"I know, but it is so hard when all of you are fit and trim and then I look at my body. I look different, like I don't belong."

"Baby girl, God designed all of us different and for different purposes. You graduated with a 4.0 and a full ride scholarship to

Verde University. None of us with our skinny selves even came close to that. You have to work with what you are given and work it. When you start looking at others and playing the comparison game that is when you get into trouble. Mya, you just have not made good eating choices. You can work on that. It is not the end of the world. Once you go to these classes, you will be fine. Our Creator is concerned about everything that concerns you, even your weight. Did you forget what Daddy always told us when we were acting like the world was gonna end and we were acting hysterical?"

I smiled, "There is nothing too hard for God. This big beautiful world was created through awesome transformative power and love, and you have access to the same power and love, use it to its fullest to create your life and dreams."

"Yes, that's it, never forget that Mya," Traci smiles as she clasps our hands together and plants tender kisses all over my face.

"I love you so much Traci, thank you."

"I love you more. Now get some rest and I'm going to make a few calls. I'll be back. Tomorrow is a new day and we are going to do this thing together, I got you."

I know that everything Traci said is right. I don't know when I started letting the weight and Paula rule me. I am kind of happy that all of this happened, now I can get myself together. How could I have forgotten that I was beautifully and wonderfully created? Even with all of the lumps and bumps, I am still God's beautiful woman, expertly designed with a purpose. My throat still hurts, and I feel exhausted, but I am thankful that things are not too bad, because it could be worse. I will look at this lesson and be grateful that I have Traci to remind me of who I am. I am beautiful and I am strong enough to face this next part of my journey and get it together.

"Lydia"

"Excuse me, Professor Triall I didn't quite get that point."
"What do you want me to do about that Ms. Swanson?"
"Repeat what you said, so I can understand, please."
"Make an appointment to see me; I can't be bothered."
The class snickers. I'm not sure what is funny. It doesn't matter anyway. I close my Women's Literature book as a sign to him that I am not pleased with him or his comment. I cross my legs and stare at him with my arms folded. I hate this class because he never takes my questions or comments seriously. You would think that someone teaching a Women's Lit class would leave his misogynist beliefs out of the curriculum, but he slips them in every single time. The clock is deliberately taunting me. When will I be free from this torture and the crackle of his monotone voice?

"Ms. Swanson," he says staring at me. His stare makes my insides quiver with intimidation; I refuse to show any fear. Ugh, I hate his almond shaped eyes and the nose hairs peeking from his nostrils.

"Yes, Mr. Triall," I answer with as much disdain as I can possibly gather together.

"That's Professor Triall, Ms. Swanson," he retorts.

I don't reply. I lock into his stare. A few seconds pass.

"Are you part of this class?"

I look around slowly and exaggerate my movements.

"It looks like it to me Professor Triall," I remark with a slight chuckle just to aggravate him.

"I strongly suggest you get your mind off of doing your laundry and what you are going to cook when you get home. Open your book and join in the class and maybe you might learn something, though the chances of that are about the same as a woman becoming president."

"You know, actually I wasn't thinking about laundry. I was thinking about how old professors go through so many mood swings and lose all their hair. Then their wives end up leaving them for vibrant and vivacious men with beautiful hair that they can run their fingers through while they make love to them."

His ears turn crimson and I shout inside as my words squeeze the life out of his heart.

31

He stands over my desk and whispers get out through his clenched teeth. I place my books inside my backpack and walk out of the room. I open the door again and yell, "Have a great day Professor Triall," and then slam it. It feels good to get back at him. It was a rumor going around campus that his wife had left him for a man that was at least twenty years younger than Professor Triall. Everyone says that's why he is so nasty to women. No one has anything good to say about him and he has been part of the faculty for over 30 years. He is the meanest man I have met in my life. I always talk back to him, in hopes that he would think twice before degrading me again. It never works; he is just crude.

It is a beautiful spring day; this is my favorite time of year. The entire campus is full of color. As I cross the street to my apartment complex, I spot Justin.

"Hey, Lydia!"

"Hi, Justin!"

"That was amazing what you did in class."

"He deserved it. I really don't like him!"

"Everyone thought it was awesome," Justin comments with a big grin.

"Well, maybe he will think twice and stop being such an idiot to women in that class. He is horrible."

"You're the only one that will say something back to him. I know that some students did write to the Dean complaining about his attitude. I'm trying to figure out why he teaches Women's Lit if he hates women so much, like give it up dude."

"He is just a confused and bitter old man. But seriously, everyone should pay me for getting them out of class early."

"Thanks Lydia, I owe you one."

"Yeah, right Justin, I will remember that," I say as I playfully nudge him. "You owe me lunch for that one!"

I was glad to get home. I turned on music to soothe my bad mood. Women's Lit is my last class for the day. Thursdays are my late classes. I usually get home by 5:30, but since I pissed off Mr. Triall or should I say Professor Triall; I'm home by 4: 45.

I have a few hours before I start my commute. My job is about an hour away. I will probably leave about 6 P.M. because I need to go to the mall and pick up a few things.

Professor Triall's face won't leave my memory. His balding head and large crimson ears seem to evade every empty space in my mind. I don't feel guilty. Well, maybe I do, but only slightly. He acts as though women shouldn't be at Bayside University and that we are only there to fill a quota. Yes, I struggled, but now I have a 3.6 GPA. I will be graduating in one semester with a B.A. in Communications. It has been quite difficult and money has been tight, but through it all I made it. One more semester and I will be a college graduate.

I dump my books and folders on the bed and stuff my backpack with some clothes, deodorant, shampoo, perfume and body glitter. I pull my hair back into a ponytail and quickly put on an orange strapless sun dress. I'm ready to go. As I drive down the street, I wonder what Professor Triall is doing. Was he thinking of me? I turn up the music a little louder and try to sing his image out of my mind. I arrive at the mall and have no problem finding a parking space. I know exactly what I'm looking for and know where to get it.

"Hi, may I help you?"

"No thanks," I reply as I make my way to the clearance rack.

There is so much to choose from and I'm surprised that they have a variety of things in small sizes. My eyes immediately light up when I see the red rhinestone ensemble. The panties are high cut bikinis trimmed in red and white rhinestones. The matching bra is just as beautiful. The bra straps are white rhinestones and it has a red rhinestone heart clasp in the front. I'm happy that it's a 38 B, perfect. My eyes scan the rack. There is a hot pink panty and bra set that is made from the sheerest material. I add it to the other five sets I've picked.

"Did you find everything?"

"Yes, thank you."

"Your total is $25.76."

"I guess I hit the jackpot," I say giving her the money.

"Thank you and have a great day," she replies.

I make it to my job without a traffic jam. I pull into the parking lot and scan the cars. It is still early, but the lot is pretty full. Even though I have been working for a year and a half, I still become jittery when there is a full house.

"Hi Lydia, how are ya? Anything interesting happened at school?" Jen asks.

"Not much," I reply as I start to change.

I didn't want to talk about Professor Triall. Even though, Jen is one of my best friends. She is beautiful; her long dark red hair shimmers with blonde highlights and her pale blue eyes are striking. We hang out sometimes after work and we look out for each other. She is a true friend.

"Lydia, I need to make a few phone calls. Can you switch with me for the first two hours tonight?" she asks.

"Yeah, no worries," I answer even though I want a few more minutes to collect my thoughts.

I quickly put the finishing touches on my eye shadow and brush my lips with a glistening streak of blue horizon lipstick, I'm ready!

I feel the heat of the lights on the back of my neck radiating down the length of my body. I listen closely to the music and pick up the beat of the drums in my hips and slowly turn around. As soon as I turn around the lights illuminate the rhinestones on my panty and bra and make a star pattern on the floor. Wow, this was a good choice; I didn't expect the rhinestones to catch the lights like this. I let the music take over every part in my body. I dip and sway as the audience becomes intoxicated with each move. I sashay to the edge of the stage and dip down to the floor and throw my chestnut brown hair forward and slowly roll my head and arch my back; then I freeze. I lock eyes with Professor Triall. He is sitting directly in front of me. He reaches out and tucks a hundred-dollar bill into my panty. My eyes water and I struggle to swallow to quench the burn in my throat. My body is stuck and I scream at every cell and nerve in my muscles to move. They don't obey me. I'm stuck in that position and can't move, iced in the moment. We both stare, refusing to look away.

"Lydia, move it, girl, what is going on? Lydia, hey Lydia" whispers Rusty, the manager, from the side of the stage.

I slowly stand. I fight to make my body move. I feel like every muscle is locked. My body and brain are disconnected. Professor Triall's eyes examine every part of my body. I'm totally humiliated! He stares into my eyes and I can't stop staring back at him. He smiles a sinister smile. I slowly part my legs into a split. We are face to face.

"You are a credit to women all over the world. You are doing the only thing that women can do," he says with a chuckle.

34

Anger sweeps through my body. I lean over the stage and I'm inches away from him. His warm breath covers my face. I smell a mixture of moth balls and cigarettes.

"You are right Professor. I get old sexually frustrated men to pay for my degree." I stand and dip one more time. A red rhinestone falls into his lap. I smile at him, unclasp my bra and throw it in the audience.

I'm ready for the music to stop. Finally, it's over, I pick the money up off the stage and make a quick exit. My mind is swirling with thoughts, none of which I understand. I look at the crumpled bills in my hands. I rush to the dressing room and unlock my locker. I stuff the money in my purse. I'm not ready to touch the bill that Professor Triall has stuck into the waistband of my panty. I wait. Slowly, I pull it out and unfold it, a hundred-dollar bill; it feels wet.

"Lydia, Lydia, why are you back here wasting time and money, get out there and mingle with the customers!" demands Rusty as he stands in the doorway.

"I'm going home for the night. Um, I'm not feeling too well."

"Whoa, hold on now, I have three parties scheduled for tonight, and one party asked for you and Stephanie, so take some aspirin and drink some water and get your tail back out there. Don't mess up my money tonight, Lydia, suck it up! I am not playing with you!"

"Not tonight Rusty, please, just leave me alone. I don't feel well," I say as I slam the locker door.

Rusty walks up to me and I step back. He gets up in my face.

"If you don't get out there and make them men happy and make'em spend some money, then don't ever come back here again. I mean it, how you gonna pay your tuition? How you gonna pay rent?"

Suddenly, I feel like I am right back in Professor Triall's class. These men are disrespecting me! How did I ever think that this was the solution? How did I resolve that I could accept this?

"Trust me, I won't need to ever walk through these doors again, I'm done! Do you understand that, creep! Don't you ever talk to me like that! I mean it!" I shout as I hurry to the exit.

My mind is swirling with pictures of the Professor, Rusty, and all the other men that have looked at me like I was nothing but an object. There was more to me than just my body. How did I get here? I am really feeling annoyed! How did I sell myself so short?

35

I have a great mind. I'm compassionate and a fantastic cook. I can make a dead party alive with my keen sense of humor. How would they know that if all they focus on are my breasts and butt? What am I doing? When did money become the controller of me?

I blocked it out and lied to myself that I was okay and that I was just doing it to get by. I was only going to dance for one semester, because my loan was denied. However, just like everything else, when I put my mind to it, I give it my all and I own it. Then it happened, each night the stage was covered with more and more money. First, just one-dollar bills and then twenty-dollar bills and then one hundred-dollar bills. Once, I made twenty-five hundred dollars in one night from a private party. Men started requesting me. I had the best dance routines. The money allowed me to have financial freedom, but was I free? I was disgusted with myself. It felt as though I had proven Professor Triall right. I was using my body and not my brain. Hmmm, all this time he knew where I worked. How many times had he been to the club? How long had he known my secret? Is this why he was so nasty to me? How many other men from campus have seen me?

This is a long drive home, alone with my accusing thoughts stabbing at me. I finally make it home and sit in the car allowing the tears to freely drip from my chin. I stop crying and become aware of a voice on the radio. A woman is talking about how Jesus died for our sins and that we can be forgiven and have a new start. I listen.

I went to church when I was a little girl, but when I graduated from high school, I thought I was too old and educated for such craziness. I continue to listen to the radio; I crave a new life. The woman continues to talk. She instructs, in such a soothing voice to repeat after her. I want to be saved. I don't want to dance anymore and fill empty afterwards. I don't want to sit on a man's lap and ignore the gold wedding band on his finger. I don't want to endure the stares penetrating my skin. I quietly repeat after her. Then the tears start to flow again, but this time it's different. I feel like I am being renewed. All of the grime from the guilt that I felt after each dance is being stripped from me. I feel refreshed. Right there in my car, an epiphany. It didn't take a big dramatic show. It was simple and personal.

I find a pen in my bag and write the number to call for prayer and to receive a free book. I wrap my arms around myself and squeeze. If He has forgiven me then I can forgive myself. I'm not going to over analyze this moment. Instead, I decide to believe.

I will not allow those experiences to make me feel bad about myself. It happened and I will move forward. I resolve that my dancing was what I felt I needed to do in that moment. Well, now I am in a new moment and the stripping won't work for me anymore. I will still keep in touch with Jen because she is a real friend that I love and care about.

Professor Triall will continue to be rude and I will continue to be the brilliant young woman that I am. If he tries to say anything to me about tonight, I will own it and speak my truth. Then, march right down to the Dean's office and file a complaint. I smile, as I remember a Bible verse, Romans 8:1 that I learned in Sunday School, there is now no condemnation for me because I am in Christ. I can't remember all of it, but I know what it means, and that is what matters. No one has the right to weigh anyone down with their judgement and that includes me. If anyone tries to judge me for it, I will not take on their opinion of me. I don't know how those experiences will impact my future, but I know that I will turn that negative energy into positivity, simply because of the lessons that I learned about other people, but more importantly what I learned about myself. Hey, what if I open a fitness studio with pole dancing classes, ha ha everyone needs a strong core and cardio.

I smile.

"Deena Rye"

"Thanks for calling, Waters and Adkins"

"May I have the accounting department?"

"Yes, hold please."

I hold the receiver away from my ear. The shrill sound of the flutes is making the pounding in my head more severe.

"Accounting, how may I help you?"

"Hi, Aubrey, it's Deena."

"Deena, you sound horrible."

"I won't be in today. Will you please let them know?"

"Not a problem, I hope you feel better."

"Thanks"

I hang up the phone and put the pillow over my head. I fall asleep for a few minutes, although I'm not really sure. Slowly, placing my feet on the floor, I stand. Suddenly, they're wet and sticky. I look down and realize I'm standing in urine and vomit. I pull the sheet off the bed and throw it on top of it. I'm straining to remember the events of last night. It is a blur. Maybe a hot shower will help. The water pounds my body and I stick my head underneath the hot stream, closing my eyes as tight as I can, while straining to recall any events of the previous night. Hmmm, nothing, but emptiness, I close my eyes again. Okay, I remember a party. Good job, now what else? Where was the party? Who was the party for? How did I get home? Who was at the party? No answers, just empty space. Suddenly, I'm aware of my hunger.

I stand in front of the refrigerator. The only things left are two slices of bacon, twelve cans of beer and a half bottle of rum. I warm the bacon in the microwave. I chew very slowly. The bacon is chewy and nasty. I slowly tiptoe back to the bedroom.

I find the remote for the television and turn it on, it is too loud. I press the mute button and watch in silence. I unwrap my hair and use the towel to clean my hands. I'm still struggling to remember last night. Leah, I remember Leah. If I call her, then maybe she can fill in the memory blanks. I reach for the phone; hell, I can't remember her number. I strain to remember the number, nothing. I can't remember.

My head is pounding; gulp, I swallow three aspirin. Then the phone starts to flash. I smile. I knew the flash mode would come in handy one day.

"Hello," I whisper into the phone.

There's nothing but laughter on the other end.

"Who is this?"

"It's Brad. You sound bad, really bad. I figured you didn't go to work today."

"Why ya say that?"

"You can't be for real. You don't remember?" Brad is still laughing.

"No, just tell me," I demand a little bit louder.

"You put on quite a show hot lady," Brad replies in a voice like you would hear on a commercial. He is too silly.

"I don't know what you are talking about. Just tell me what happened. I have been busting my brain to remember and the only thing I know is that I was at a party."

"Yep, first clue, look in your purse and see if that helps you out," Brad is still using that silly voice.

I dump my purse out in front of me. There are crumpled up dollar bills and a lot of quarters. Now I'm even more puzzled. My head swirls. Where did this come from?

"Brad, tell me what happened," I plead with a slight quiver in my voice.

"After your drinking binge, you said that you would do cartwheels for quarters or insults. Then, Dynamite Deena put on an insult show. Brad let the "D" roll off his tongue in such dramatic fashion.

I'm speechless. I'm stunned. I'm confused. I'm annoyed. I'm pissed. I'm about to cuss him out!

"Please tell me that you are lying, Brad. Don't play with me, damn it, don't play with me Brad! Stop, being silly. I am so serious right now, so serious!"

"Trust me, I am not lying. You were quite the entertainer."

"Who gave me money? Who was at the party? Why didn't you stop me?" I am trying to concentrate on Brad's voice and not the banging in my head.

"I don't know; I left the patio and went inside."

40

I close my eyes and strain to concentrate. I need to remember! Nothing happens, I remember nothing. My memory is erased.

"I was just about to call Leah before you called, so she could tell me what happened. She was at the party, right, Leah was there?"

"That wouldn't be a good idea. Don't call her! Deena Rye, you really don't remember what happened. Are you serious?" Brad sounds like he doesn't believe me.

"Brad, I'm seriously not faking, tell me."

"Maybe you need some help. You always do this. Well, Leah isn't talking to you. The two of you got into a yelling match. You told her that she was jealous of your body and that no one would pay a penny to see her dance topless with her sagging flabby breasts. Then you said some more stuff which I am not gonna say. Because DR, you were doing too much and saying too much!"

"No, no I didn't say that," I utter in disbelief.

"Yep, ya did. I was there, trust and believe you said it."

Leah has been trying to lose weight since she gave birth to Emily. She is so worried about her shape. How could I say that to her and not even remember it? How could I be so rude to my dear friend?

"You ruined Leah's party. Not to mention that you insulted her in her house and in front of her friends. You did go too far, even for you. At least you got change for the meter," Brad says with a laugh.

"How many cartwheels and insults did I do?"

"I think just a few, because Leah stopped you and that's why you started yelling at her. But, for the rest of the night some guys just kept on throwing quarters at you, for a joke. And you kept on picking them up and doing cartwheels. You know, this kind of reminds me of when we went to Mardi Gras. You were way out there!"

"I can't remember!" I scream into the phone.

"Deena Rye everyone is getting pretty sick of you getting drunk and then pretending like you don't remember. You know you remember. It is not funny anymore."

"You stupid idiot, I don't remember! Do you think I am making it all up? Are you dumb or something? Yea, you are dumb and stupid and a liar! I hate you!"

"You have a problem, DR."

Brad hung up on me. Everyone is mad at me. I put the money back in the purse. I want to know who had given me the money. The

41

only people at the party were a few of her neighbors and some family members. Why was she mad at me? She should have been mad at them for giving me money. She shouldn't have let me have too much to drink. My head hurts and I have cotton mouth. I tiptoe into the kitchen and grab the bottle of rum. I swallow a few gulps and put it back in the refrigerator. I didn't want to think about stupid Leah or her stupid party or her stupid friends. Within an hour, I finish three of the beers and the rest of the rum. I am feeling much better. That's what I needed, a few drinks.

It's about 2:00 in the afternoon when I decide to talk to Leah. I pick up the phone and struggle to remember her number. I need to make her understand. I finally remember she is speed dial 3, really Deena girl, you forgot. I can't get through because she has blocked my number. I try to dial again and again. I continue to get the same message. I throw the phone against the wall. I must talk to her to apologize. Brad can get her to talk to me. I just hope that he is not mad and will pick up the phone.

"Brad, it's me, Deena and please don't hang up."

"Yeah, what you want, talk quick."

I start sobbing. I can't even remember why I called.

"Deena Rye stop it, get a hold of yourself," Brad demands.

"I can't. I don't know what is wrong with me."

"You have a problem. It's just that simple. You need to call an alcohol or drug abuse hotline and get help. Everyone is sick of this and I guess it is time you do something about it. We have all tried to help you. You have to be serious this time, you can't quit the treatment, like you always do. You can't do it by yourself; there is nothing wrong with getting help. If you don't get help, then you are going to be all alone. I'll come over in a little while and we will call them together."

"Thank you, Brad, I love you. I will see you later."

I look in the mirror. I'm pathetic. How did I get to this point? How was I going to get out of this mess? Brad is right for once in his life. Well, maybe he is wrong. I can do it my way. I don't need anyone helping me. I got in this mess by myself and I can get out by myself. I am going to clean myself up and prove to everyone that I can do it. I don't need to go to a therapist and tell them my problems. I am smart enough to do it on my own, I will stop drinking and that is all I have to do, so there. I can do this. It ain't that hard.

I still need to talk to Leah. I must apologize to her and let her know that I'm going to stop, no more empty promises. I am truly going to miss the taste and the smell of alcohol, but this is it. I have to change my life or lose the few people that are still in my life.

I will go over to Leah's house since she won't accept my phone calls. I'm not exactly sure of what to say, but I know that I have to force her to forgive me. I am making her give me another chance. I still am trying to remember the party, but it's just an irritating void. Well, I will just tell her that I am sorry and that I'm getting help. I will cry and hug her and everything will be fine. Whew, I feel better already, this is the perfect plan!

My stomach flips and shivers the entire time I am driving to Leah's house. What if she doesn't open the door? What if she calls the police on me? I'll just have to chance it. Brad and Leah are the last of my friends. Brad, actually is my cousin, but he is still a friend. All the other ones have abandoned me, because I always drink too much and then say too much or do too much. Last night, it seems as though I did both, said and did too much.

I drive into the parking lot of the convenience store. I need a little something to settle my nerves before I talk to Leah. Slowly, walking to the back of the store, I spot a six pack of beer. The cans feel cool and little trickles of water slide down the cans. A small sign reads two bottles of wine for five dollars. I pick up two. This is a bargain, and besides I might as well have a few drinks because this is the last shebang. I pay for the beer and wine with the quarters and crumpled dollar bills. My cartwheel and insult routine came in handy.

As I am figuring out the plan, I gulp down two beers. I'm so thirsty! It's a good thing I'm only a few blocks away from Leah's house. Suddenly, it pops in my mind. Am I stupid? How can I apologize to her about getting drunk, and then have beer on my breath? She will be really pissed and will yell at me again. There must be something that will mask the alcohol smell on my breath.

I go back in the store and buy a jumbo garlic pickle and a bag of onion cheddar pretzels. Garlic and onion will definitely hide the smell of beer. These pretzels are dry and make me thirstier. I unscrew the cap off the wine and take several long gulps, hmm, kind of tasty for five bucks. Within a few minutes, the bottle is empty. I feel pretty

43

confident! Crunch, slurp, two more huge bites of the pickle. The juice runs down my arm. The seasonings on the pickle taste so good. I chug another beer. The front seat is full of empty beer cans.

Stop it! What is wrong with me? Immediately, I am overwhelmed by frustration and anger. I put the car in drive and zoom out of the parking lot. Leah is critical to helping me. If she won't let me in her house, maybe, at least she will talk to me outside. Staring at the cans and bottle, I reach down, pick up a can and slam it against the dashboard and then throw it in the back seat. I reach down and grab another can; suddenly the air is filled with honking horns. I look up and two cars are headed towards me.

I'm in the wrong lane! I jerk the steering wheel; the car starts to violently spin. I can't grab the wheel. I scream and close my eyes! The air fills with screeching, screaming, grinding steel and a mosaic of colors. My head plummets into the windshield and an intense burning fills my head. My body is being torched. Every part of my skin itches, tingles, and stretches. My body is weightless; I fly. The pin pricking sensations underneath my fingernails are concentrated. My head bobs and swings from side to side, then forward and back. I'm a pendulum! The bitter taste of blood coats my tongue and fills my mouth. My gums release their teeth. Then, there is nothing but silence and darkness, fade to black.

I attempt to move my body, but I can't. There is a keen awareness of pain. A pain that none of my nerves have experienced before, a pain that stabs and assaults my body. Everything inside of me is roaring for the pain to slow down, but it races throughout my body with great force and speed. With each second the pain intensifies and my body is battered more and more. I try to open my eyes, but they won't open. My ears try to decipher the tones and shrills of sounds, and my brain tries to connect with my ears, but it's not happening. The only thing that my brain knows is debilitating pain. Then, miraculously it happens. My ears recognize Leah's voice. Yes, Leah! She came to see about me. I demand my eyes to open! I comprehend white and light. It is the type of white that you see on ER shows. Hey, my brain and eyes are connecting; I'm in a hospital. My eyes immediately shut. Leah came to see me in the hospital. I can always count on her. Finally, I will be able to talk to her.

"Let me in there now!" Leah screams over and over.

Yes, I hope someone lets her in to talk to me.

"Brad, let me go! Let me go! No, let me in there!" Leah yells with force and determination.

Brad is here, this is perfect. We can all talk and work this out together. I demand my eyes to open again and they do. The room is too bright, eyes shut. Come on brain, tell my eyes to open!

"Leah, please, Leah please!" Brad yells. His voice is distressed.

"Ugh, no, let go, I said let go. Let go! Let me in! I swear!"

There's a loud crash. Leah bursts through the door. Brad pulls her back by her shirt and yells for help. I try to reach out to her, but I can't. I'm handcuffed to the bed. Police run through the door and try to pull Leah out of the room. I see her eyes and they shoot through me. I've never seen such a wild look in anyone's eyes. It scares me. I'm terrified. What's wrong with her? I have never felt this before.

"You killed Emily! You killed my baby! You killed her! Emily is dead! Emily is dead! My baby is dead! She's gone! Dead! Dead! Emily is dead!" She screeches as she claws and thrashes to reach the bed. Her arms are straining to reach me. Her eyes are wide and scarlet. Veins are popping from her neck, as if they will erupt from underneath her skin. I don't know the voice that is coming from her mouth, it is between a bellow and scream and deep agonizing pain. She claws at the air. Brad is pulling her, trying to hold her. Several police demand that a nurse comes now. It's extreme chaos!

The police and Brad struggle to carry her out of the room. I'm confused. My mind churns and I attempt to focus. How could I have possibly killed Emily? Leah is crazy. What happened, how did Emily die? When did Emily die? I love her, why would I kill her? Before I can even figure it out, other police enter the room.

"Deena Rye Nelson, you have been charged with vehicular homicide while under the influence of alcohol. You caused an accident which resulted in the death of Ms. Emily Dixon," the officer states with total disgust. He hates me. They are all gawking at me.

"No, no, no, no, shut up! How, shut up! No!" I repeat over and over and over and over and over and over and over. It's over!

"Yes, you loser, you should be dead, not an innocent baby. You better be glad it was them and not me. I would have let her go," she says glaring at me.

I close my eyes and scream! It is too late to get help. My

choices are now fatal consequences. The word choices reverberate through my eardrum and that is all I can hear, choices, choices. I made the choice to pretend that I did not have a problem. All my friends walked out of my life because I was unreliable, crude, and lied. I convinced myself that they were all flawed and I was perfect. I never was reflective; the only reflection that I participated in was the kind of reflecting on the good old days and ignoring the current bad old days. It is easy to build a fake reality when you ignore accountability, wise counsel and sit comfortably in the space of waiting for the right moment. Knowing full well that the right moment has shown up consistently each time, but I intentionally pushed it out of the way as I sat in the comfort of dysfunction.

It's too late! My denial has caused death, mine and Emily's. I scream, fade to doom.

"Amber"

It was finally my turn. My Pastor stood in front of me holding a beautiful gilded large Bible.

"Please raise your right hand and place your left hand on the Bible and repeat after me. I take this vow as witnessed by the Father, Son, Holy Spirit and this congregation."

I raise my trembling right hand and repeat after him.

"God Bless you Sister Amber Taylor."

He takes a purple box off the silver tray that the Deacon is holding. I open it and place the silver band with an engraved heart on my finger. The congregation stands and claps. We face them and walk back to our seats. We smile at each other because we just shared a sacred moment. As the Pastor gives the benediction I look down at my ring and close my eyes. Lord, help me to keep my vow, I whisper. Before I open my eyes, I feel my Mom's hug.

"We are so proud of you. You don't know how happy we are!"

"Let me see the ring," Dad says reaching for my hand, "this is absolutely wonderful Amber. I am so happy for you."

"I feel that this is right for me." I reply smiling at my parents.

"It most certainly is," Dad agrees still holding my hand.

"Even though you are thirty it is never too late to become celibate," Mom adds looking at the ring and then at me. She is pleased.

"You are right," I say as I nod in agreement.

I have decided to be part of our church's celibacy group. We had an entire month of Bible studies and workshops to prepare us to take our vows. It was very intense, but worth it.

There are fifty people in the group. The group is made up of various ages, from teens to senior citizens. We vow not to have sex until we marry and to wear our bands to symbolize our commitment.

When I told my parents about my decision to be part of the group, they were very pleased. Mom was ecstatic. I've had four sexual partners. My last boyfriend cheated on me eight times, with five different women. I always took him back and believed that he would change. I even thought I could change him if I loved him harder. Nope, he lied to me each time. I didn't learn my lesson until I went for my annual pap smear and my doctor told me that I had contracted Chlamydia. I was in total shock. I broke up with him, although he tried to convince me that the doctor had mixed up the test with someone else's. He said he only screwed around with clean girls and that's why he didn't use condoms. What, really? His explanation was the dumbest thing I had ever heard. From that moment on I knew that sex wasn't something that I should take lightly and that I could get a STI, yes, unprotected sex could have life altering consequences.

I walk in my house and see the red light blinking on the phone. Yes, I still have an old-fashioned landline and answering machine, as a backup in case something happens to my cell phone. I press the button and walk in the kitchen to get a soda. Todd left a message; I call him without hesitation.

"Would you like to go to dinner?"

"How did you know it was me? I didn't even say anything," I ask somewhat shocked, yet intrigued.

"You have a special ring tone."

"Well, that's cute," I say with a chuckle, "I am flattered."

Todd and I have been dating for almost three months. I met him at the grocery store. We both happened to be on the cereal aisle at the same time, both trying to grab a box of Sunny Morning Triple Oatmeal Crunch.

"You didn't answer my question. Would you like to go to dinner? I miss you."

"Sure, let's go to the Sunset Grille."

"Sounds like a plan to me. Are you ready now or do you need a few minutes?" Todd asks with excitement in his voice.

"Leave your place in about fifteen minutes and I will be ready when you get here. Yes, that should be enough time, can't wait."

I am excited to see him; I miss him. We both have been busy.

"See you then, bye."

"Bye"

I look down at my hand again and smile. Everything is going well with Todd, but for some strange reason I haven't told him about my decision to be celibate. Truthfully, I am kind of scared of his response. However, I am not going to compromise my beliefs anymore. In the back of my mind, a little voice screams that Todd is going to leave as soon as I tell him. Stop, I am not focusing on that

48

right now. He will be here in a few minutes. I wash my face and apply some more lipstick. I decide to change into something more comfortable. I put on a sundress and spritz on some perfume. As I rub lotion on my hands, I take off the ring. I'm not ready to have this conversation. I place it in the jewelry box, and immediately guilt stands up in my heart.

As I wait for Todd, I check the calendar to see what is scheduled for Monday. A 10:00 AM appointment with the Diabetes Fundraiser Coordinator. I'm a party planner for Festive Creations. My creative vibe is responsible for some of the most elaborate parties and receptions in the state of South Carolina.

Whew, I am trying to ignore the guilt and just when I am about to go back to the jewelry box, the doorbell chimes.

"Hi Amber," Todd greets me with a hug.

"Hi"

"Are you ready?"

"Almost, let me grab my purse and I'll meet you in the car."

As I pick up the purse, it feels like a blanket is weighing me down, the cloak of shame. I've taken a solemn vow in front of God and my church family. I will not be ashamed. I quickly go to the jewelry box and remove the ring, then place it in my purse.

The Sunset Grille is one of my favorite restaurants. Our dinner is delicious and we have an engaging conversation. That's one of the reasons I like Todd so much; he is diverse. We talk about sports, home renovations, stocks, yoga poses and all the stupid stuff we did as kids. He is wonderful! Why wouldn't he honor my decision? Gosh, am I over thinking this?

Todd interrupts my thoughts, "Wanna take a walk on the beach?"

"Sure"

The sun is about to set and the sky is a mixture of lavender, pink and blue. It's amazingly serene and pretty.

"Isn't the sky, beautiful?"

"It sort of looks like cotton candy," I reply tilting my head all the way back, "you know the big jumbo bags at the state fair."

"Yeah, you're right. I never thought of the sky as cotton candy," Todd says with a slight grin.

I smile widely, "Hang with me, you will learn something new

every day. I will have you seeing all kind of things."

We walk out to the dock and sit down. Todd holds my hand as we stare out at the water and watch the Sea Gulls effortlessly glide above us. Todd is watching me, but I continue to stare straight ahead. He pulls me closer to him and kisses me. I don't respond. He gently kisses my lips again, and still, I refuse to respond.

"What's the matter?" he asks as he drops my hand.

"I'm fine," I reply, making sure not to look at him.

He looks at me, "You definitely have something going on up there. Amber, talk to me. What's up with you?"

"I'm just thinking about how beautiful the sky is and the rippling of the waves is kind of hypnotizing me, just having a quiet moment. That's all, it's nothing."

Todd stands and reaches for my hand and pulls me to my feet. He pulls me close and I smell his cologne. Wow, he smells so good. I want to kiss his neck. Chill out Amber, I tell myself.

"May I kiss you?" he asks.

"Yes"

I am awakened in the moment. Todd is a great kisser. He doesn't rush and it doesn't feel like he is trying to swallow my tongue or drown me with his saliva. Hold up, I am enjoying this too much. I open my eyes and step back from him. I take a deep breath, whoa exhale girl, get it together. My heart beat is going a little bit too fast and the butterflies in my stomach are fluttering and everywhere else is fluttering. I remember my oath.

"Um, it's time to go," I back away from him, even though my flesh is screaming at me and begging me to stay to get one more kiss.

"I agree," Todd says and walks away.

I'm not sure if he is mad or disappointed. I wonder why he didn't try to convince me to stay. Oh, well I am glad he didn't. Just like the Bible says I was given an exit out of this temptation, yes, whew, thank you Jesus, cause you already know, what was about to happen.

Todd holds my hand as he drives back to my house. He's in deep thought. This feels awkward; we ride in silence.

"Do you mind if I come in for a minute?" he asks.

I guess he is breaking it off with me, and this will be the goodbye speech. I hate break up talks. I feel kind of sad because I

50

really like him a lot. At least I don't have to get into the whole celibacy thing with him. That is a slight sense of relief, since I know, he will be ready to take it to another level. We have never had sex, but we've some intense kissing sessions. However, we never made it to the bedroom. Which is good, I can't miss what I never had, but I will be missing those kisses! C'mon be real you know those good kissers are hard to find.

"Would you like something to drink?" I ask trying to remain calm, but there is a slight edge in my voice.

"No, I'm fine," he says as he sits on the sofa.

I hope he doesn't drag this out, just say it and go. I'm practicing my reaction in my head. I have decided to stay calm and act like it's not a big deal. I'll tell him that I have been thinking about calling things off. Although, if I am going to be honest, it is a huge deal and I am ticked off. I was starting to love Todd, but I'm going to play it cool. I am Ms. No Drama Amber. Alright, let's get this over with so I can keep it moving.

"Amber, I have enjoyed these few months. You have become more than a friend to me. About a month ago, I made a very important decision that I didn't share with you. I'm not sure why I didn't talk to you about it. Maybe, I just wasn't ready to talk about it, but it's something that you need to know."

I'm looking straight at him and not even blinking. If he says he started dating his ex, I'm going to be so mad. I won't be cool if that is what comes out of his mouth. He told me all about her craziness. Is he leaving me for that? He must be crazy stupid. Trust and believe I am going OFF, on him! If he says that, then I will bring out Ms. Don't Try Me Amber in full force!

"Oh really, and what decision would that be?" I try to keep my voice low and calm. It is difficult. I am waiting for him to say Liza and it is on. I will give him all the words! Let me say this, I love the Lord, but I will still check you.

"First, I want to say that I hope we can find some type of compromise and reach a mutual understanding."

Todd stands up and puts his hand in his pocket. He pulls his hand out of his pocket and turns his back to me. Then, he turns back around and holds out his hand.

"Shh, don't say anything," I instruct him with a sigh of relief.

51

I walk over to my purse and take out my ring and slip it on my finger. I turn toward him and hold out my hand to him. Our rings are identical! He grabs me and plants small tender kisses all over my face. My heart soars!

"When did you get this?" he asks grinning and shaking his head in disbelief.

"This morning, and I've been fighting with myself about how I was going to tell you that I have taken a celibacy vow. I didn't know how to bring it up. Babe, I was so nervous."

"This is incredible! Amber, this is so right!"

Todd clasps his hands together and says thank you Lord, over and over again. There is an authentic praise happening.

"Now that the hard part is over, there is one more thing that I need to say," Todd says with a huge smile.

"Don't tell me that you have been keeping more secrets from me," I say playfully and pat him on the back.

"I want us to date each other exclusively. Amber, I love you more and more each day. I can't stop thinking about you. When I think about my future you are in it. When I think about fathering kids, I want you to be their mom. I want you to be my wife. I want a family with you. You make me a better me. I want to be in a position to help you reach your goals. I am falling hard and this time I am not scared to love another person. You make saying I love you easy and fearless."

"Babe, I feel the same way."

"So, does that mean yes. It's me and you?" Todd asks with jubilation.

"I want you to be mine. I was trying to be reserved when you said you had something to say. I thought you were about to tell me you were getting back with Liza. I was trying to act cool, but I was getting heated and was about to let you have it. I don't want you with anybody else, just me and you. I want you to be my forever love."

Todd scoops me up in his arms, "You are the answer to my prayers. You have no idea. I have found my treasure, it's you."

"And God answered my prayers and sent you, my way!"

"This is so incredible. I have been participating in the Bible for Bros Group at my church. There was a lesson about purity and celibacy, afterwards, a few of us got together with our Pastor and started talking about it. Then, we purchased these rings as a symbol of our commitment to God and future families."

"I am so happy for you Todd. One day you are going to be a fantastic husband and dad."

"Likewise, you are going to be an amazing wife and mommy. I believe I have found my good thing and it's you, Amber."

I stand in the moment thinking and having a praise break in my heart, as I envision becoming Todd's wife. I know with God and trust as the foundation of our relationship, we will be able to overcome the storms and love each other through the rough times. I am not afraid.

"Todd, I love you."

"Amber I love you," he says as he gently kisses the back of my hand.

We hold each other in such a tender and caring embrace. Standing there, hugging my future husband and father to my future kiddos. The person that will support me when I want to give up and the person that I will commit to love for better and worse, because the worse will come. However, we'll figure it out and protect our bond. My heart has craved this type of love for a long time. I am able to be vulnerable and strong. I almost gave up on love after the horrible relationships that I had. It was difficult to wait, but I knew that at the right time the universe was going to bring him to me, if there was room for love in my heart. Clearing the clutter of betrayal and hurt, was step number one, then consistent meditation and prayer. I had to discipline my will to wait and now I have Todd.

"Cassandra"

I step off the bus and immediately put on my jacket. My husband, Tyler, insists that I wear a jacket to stop other men from looking at me. It's about ninety degrees, but I wear a jacket year-round, the temperature doesn't matter. I jog home because I can't be late; he hates it when I'm late.

As I enter the house, I quietly close the door. Even though he's not home yet, I am trained not to make unnecessary noise. I change my clothes and make sure that my ponytail is neat. He loves my long hair and always wants me to wear it in a neat slick ponytail. Tyler's happiness is the only thing that matters to me.

I start dinner, then glance at the clock, if I'm lucky I will have an hour to myself. I turn on the TV and place the remote on Tyler's chair. He will strangle me if he knew that I was watching TV without his permission. A car door slams; I hurriedly turn off the TV and run into the kitchen. Holding my breath, waiting for the front door to open, but it never does. My breathing regulates itself and I decide not to take any more chances. I stay in the kitchen until I complete dinner. My heart can't take the anxiety.

I run upstairs and put Tyler's pajamas on the bed and make his bubble bath. I check the water's temperature with a thermometer, it must be exactly right.

"Sandi, I'm home!"

I stand at the top of the stairs waiting for him to come around the corner. Please let him be in a good mood. I hear his footsteps approaching and my breathing quickens and my face twitches.

"Hello Tyler, your bath is ready," I announce as pleasantly as possible. I don't want him to hear the nervousness in my inflection. He kisses me on the hand and walks in the bedroom.

"What's for dinner?"

"Spaghetti and garlic bread," I reply in a monotone voice.

I wait. He doesn't respond. Oh no, did I pick out the wrong thing for dinner? He walks pass me and slowly walks in the bathroom. He closes the door. I stand in the hall as he swishes the water to test the temperature. About three minutes pass and I am terrified.

"Is everything fine?" I ask, walking closer to the door.

"Yeah, you may leave now."

"Tyler, thank you, I'm here to please only you."

I'm overjoyed that everything is great. I'm not allowed to move until he checks the temperature and say that I am here to please him. Sometimes, he will change what reply he wants me to use, but he tells me in advance and then I have one day to learn it.

I prepare our plates and sit at the table. I breathe a little easier, because so far things are going well. He comes down the stairs in his pajamas. Whew, no frowns or signs of agitation.

"When were these washed?" he asks as he sniffs the sleeve.

"A week ago," I answer looking down at the plate.

"They don't smell that fresh. I can't smell the fabric softener."

I lower my head even more, trying to think of what to say.

"Do you hear me talking to you, Sandi!" he yells as he grabs my ponytail and wraps it around his hand. My head snaps back.

"Yes Tyler, I will do better. I'm sorry."

"Does this smell fresh to you?" he asks still holding my hair and burying my face into his stomach. "Do you smell that? Is this fresh Sandi? Do you think this is good enough? Do you like that smell? What do you smell? Do you smell any fragrance, huh?"

"No, it's not, it's not fresh," I say trying to say it loud enough for him to hear, but my face is still pressed against his stomach. I can barely breathe or speak; his large fat stomach is muffling my voice.

He pulls me up out of the chair by my hair. I close my eyes and hold my breath. He tightens the grip, and my scalp stings, eyes water, and my heart pounds.

"Cassandra, how many times have I told you about my pajamas? You still can't get it right! You are the dumbest woman I have ever seen! Aren't you? Aren't you, dumb?"

"Yes, Tyler, yes, I am the dumbest woman. I can't do anything right. I don't know why you put up with me, yes, I am stupid," I say while starting to cry and tremble.

He takes off the pajama shirt and balls it up with one hand. Then, wipes my face with it. He still has a tight grip on the ponytail. He has wound my hair around his hand.

"This is all this shirt is good for, to wipe the tears of a dumb idiot! Let me wipe your face for you, since you want to cry!"

He scrubs my face harder and harder. My face burns and stings as he continues to scrub it with the cotton shirt. Suddenly, he stops and throws the shirt on the floor. My head snaps back, I am looking up at him. He shakes his head in disgust. His mouth is moving but I can't hear what he is saying.

"Our dinner is ruined! Do you expect me to eat cold spaghetti?"

"I'll warm it for you," I reply trying to sound as loving as possible. It's hard to do, because of the burning sensation covering my face and the pain that's dancing and twirling around my scalp.

"I don't want warmed up food! It must be fresh, start over!"

"Yes, Tyler I live to please only you." I manage to say through tears and excruciating pain.

He releases my hair from his clutch and walks over to the stove. Tyler dumps all the food in the garbage, including what I had on the plates. Then he throws the plates in the sink.

"Start over!" he demands with fiery rage.

My heart almost explodes through my chest. I can't catch my breath. There isn't any more spaghetti! I cooked the whole box. I stand in front of the garbage can staring at the spaghetti.

"Tyler, I need to go to the store."

I close my eyes and try to steady myself for the hit. I wait.

"The store! I'm supposed to wait and starve because you didn't prepare the meal right. You are supposed to get enough food when I take you to the store. I'm in my pajamas and now you want me to go to the store!" he shakes his head as if he can't believe what is happening. He paces back and forth, pacing faster and faster with each step. Now Tyler mumbles and throws his hands up in the air. He stops.

I stand motionless. He walks over to me and slaps me with such force that I fall over the garbage can and land on the floor. Tyler picks up some of the spaghetti off the floor and smashes it in my face.

"Get up! Get up! Get up! Stand up! Stand up now!"

I cover my face and start to cry. He yanks me up by my ponytail and I am sure that I hear my hair separate from the scalp. His fist pounds into my jaw. I'm trying to crawl away, but he pulls me back by my legs. The fist lands on my nose.

"I'm so sick of you! Why did I marry you? How could I marry the dumbest good for nothing loser! Why do I even try? I give you everything! Why do you make me so mad?" he yells.

Tyler drags me to the stairs. I try to kick, but his grip is too tight. He walks backwards up the steps, as he drags and pulls me up each stair. My back feels like its spine is going to pop out through my lower back. The carpet burns my skin. My head bobbles and slams against each stair. I scream. He doesn't notice. Finally, we get to the top landing of the stairs. He picks me up and throws me on our bedroom's floor. There's a loud crack from my shoulder.

"Tyler please, please stop, I love you and I'm sorry," I yell, trying to connect to him, "I'm sorry. Tyler, you are right! I love you! Tyler sweetheart! Honey, I will fix it, I promise!"

It is no use, he's in his zone and he won't stop until he becomes exhausted from kicking and punching my body. I use to fight back, but it only made him madder and the beatings longer. About a year ago, I decided to take the beatings just to get them over with as quickly as possible. But this beating is lasting too long. It feels like I'm going to pass out from the pain. My body is shutting down.

He walks over to the closet and snatches a pair of pants off a hanger. I attempt to run out the room; he grabs me by the back of my neck and throws me to the floor. The wooden pants hanger slams across my back and face, leaving open wounds with each hit. I reach up and grab it. Tyler looks surprise and for a second, he stands still. Neither one of us can believe that I'm fighting back. I kick him as hard as I can. Honestly, I can't tell you where this is coming from. What is wrong with me? I must be delirious.

"What da hell? You must be crazy! You hit me! Are you out of your mind?" he sounds confused and shocked. Tyler pauses and looks up at the ceiling, as if he is trying to figure out the next move.

I jump up and run out of the room and into the bathroom, slamming and locking the door. I am amazed. What in the world am I thinking? What's next? He is right I've lost my mind. I've flipped out! What now? Ugh, think, what can I do?

"Open this door!" he yells while kicking the door.

I look around for something to use to protect myself for when the door falls down. It will be a matter of minutes before the door crashes in on me. I see the telephone on the dirty clothes hamper. He had forgotten the phone in the bathroom. I pick it up and dial 911.

"I'm going to kill you, Cassandra! You are dead! Tonight, you

58

die! Yes, that is it, I am going to kill you!"

I hastily explain the situation to the operator, and she assures me that the police are on the way. I start to cry and shake. I lose all control. Tyler is coming back up the stairs. Then, I remember, the gun is downstairs. Did he go downstairs to get the gun? Within seconds, I realize he is really going to kill me. I am going to die, tonight. I can barely see because my eyes are almost completely swollen shut. I tell the operator that he has a gun and I'm going to die. I know this is the end of my life. I express it's too late. What does death feel like? Will I die quickly or slowly? Will there be a bright light? How much pain will I feel from the bullet penetration?

"You have disrespected me for the last time! I'm going to give you one more chance to open this door or I will shoot it off! Do you hear me, Cassandra? I will shoot this door down and then shoot you! 1,2, Sandra! Open it! Now! 3,4! Cassandra! I told you about disobeying me! This is the last time!"

I hold the phone to my ear and strain to listen to the operator; she's telling me something, but I can't interpret it. Once again, she assures me that the police will be here soon and for me not to open the door. Tonight, I'm going to heaven. I tell the operator that he is going to shoot me. But you know what, I'm not afraid to die. At least I will be safe. I pray out loud and ask Jesus to save me from death, but if Tyler shoots me, I ask Jesus to quickly take me to heaven.

"Cassandra! Open this door!" he kicks the door and I hear a loud cracking noise. The bottom hinge pops halfway off. Then it happens, Tyler fires the gun. AHHH! I'm closer to death. Wailing and trembling I pick up the phone again. The operator shouts my name.

"Cassandra, listen to me, is there a window in the bathroom?"

"Yes, but I am upstairs," I say as I stand and walk to the window. "Jesus, help me! Help me Jesus!" I holler over and over. I am hollering as loud as I can.

"You need to get out of there, jump out of the window. The police are a few blocks away," her voice is calm but urgent.

She's right; I'm not dead yet, so why not die trying to save my life. I have a window! Tyler is screaming at me. This door will plummet down any second. I climb out the window and hang on to the ledge; suddenly the area is covered with red and blue lights. The door crashes to the floor; I let go of the ledge. I hit the ground and my legs twist underneath me. I lay still trying to figure out if I am dead or alive. A gunshot cracks the air. I am alive! Tyler leans out the window and is shooting at me. Someone grabs me and scoops me in his arms.

"You're safe now."

"Give her back! She belongs to me!" Tyler screams.

I pull myself up from behind the car to see what's happening. Tyler points the gun at a police car. My vision is blurry. A man forces my head back down behind the car. I lay flat on the ground. The asphalt is hard against my skin and I smell motor oil.

"Drop your weapon!"

The air is saturated with yells.

"Give her back to me! You have nothing to do with this! She belongs to me! She can't live without me! Sandi! Sandra! Cassandra!" he yells waving his gun back and forth at the police cars. The police demand Tyler to drop his weapon.

"No one tells me what to do! Cassandra, come back!"

Shots collide with yells and I hear Tyler's screams. I pop my head back up, as I strain to see through swollen eyes. It happens. He puts the gun to his head and fires. I can't believe it. He did it. Tyler killed himself. Just like that, he is gone.

I faint.

"Cassandra, you are in the ambulance and we are going to take you to the hospital, and you're safe."

I didn't care that they were taking me to the hospital; I just concentrated on the word safe. I had not felt safe in years. He is dead and I can't even cry. Sadness covers me, but I can't even explain why. I finally make it to the hospital and they start treating me. After many hours of rest and trying to figure out which emotion I should hold on to, I pick confusion. My mind is looping.

"Cassandra, how are you feeling?" asks the nurse as she checks my blood pressure.

"I'm not sure," I murmur. It's difficult to talk; my mouth feels like it weighs over a hundred pounds.

"The swelling should go down soon. Would you like a cold pack? That may make you more comfortable. We are just going to keep you on liquids for the rest of the day and then maybe tomorrow we will start you on some soft foods."

I gently shake my head to let her know that I understand what she is telling me.

"Someone from the police department and a Social Worker will be in to see you later. I told them that you would probably sleep for a while and to come back later. You need more rest, even though you slept through the night."

I nod. It's a new day. I can't believe it. I slept through the night.

"Sweetheart, you are going to be just fine," she reassures me with a gentle smile.

"My husband, is he dead?" I mumble.

"From the information that I was given, yes he is," she answers as she fills a cup with ice chips. "Try to put a piece in, honey, your mouth won't feel dry."

She gently pries open my mouth and slips in a small chip of ice. Yes, it feels good melting in my mouth. I nod my head to signal that I like it and want more. She slips in another piece.

I can't remember the last time someone had taken care of me. For so long I only focused on Tyler. I wasn't allowed to have contact with my family or friends; there was no one to take care of me. My world was Tyler. Now, someone is taking care of me, even if it is a nurse and it's her job. She's nice and caring and even though I appreciate her, it feels strange.

"Sweetheart, now you can start a new life. You are going to get well and you are going to be just fine. I know it is none of my business, but why did you stay there and take this? Oh wait, don't answer that. Forgive me, I shouldn't be asking that anyway and I don't want you to talk, just rest and get well."

I shouldn't talk, but I feel compelled to answer her. In this moment I need her, she is more than a nurse.

"He was my husband," I whisper, "he is all I had. I had to obey him. He was my," a pain shoots through my jaw and I can't talk.

She slips another ice chip between my lips.

"Yes, he was your husband, but that didn't give him the right to beat you. He almost killed you, no one has the right to do that." she just looks at me. "Just because he married you, didn't mean that he could do whatever he wanted to you. A husband should love and support you, not try to rule over you and beat you. Cassandra, you did not deserve that; he was wrong."

Though it's difficult to talk with engorged lips I want to continue to talk to her; I'm connecting with her and feel that she has been purposed in this moment for me. I need to make sense of all of this. I need reassurance that it's going to be fine. Can I survive? Tyler is gone; I am alone. Will my parents even talk to me? I haven't seen them in years. I don't have any friends. I only had Tyler and he only had me.

"He loved me."

I'm not sure if I am making a statement or asking a question. I want her to answer, I'm trying to figure this out. Did he love me?

"No, that is not love. Have you ever read, 1 Corinthians 13:4-7? It tells us about love. That is the example that we should use for love. It is not about gifts, keeping score, beating up each other physically or verbally, no it is beautiful and kind, caring, and compassionate. If that is the example that we are to follow, how can he beat you and say he loves you? That was not love, far from it, trust me. When you get a chance read it."

Her eyes are so full of gentleness and I can tell that she really wants me to get it.

"Don't let anyone abuse you, whether it is a man or woman. Love doesn't seek to hurt or cause pain. Now you rest, and I will come back to check in on you. But if you need anything, just press this button," she slips another ice chip between my lips and smiles at me.

"Thanks," I mutter. I focus on the coolness of the chip. For once, in a long time I focus on what is going on inside of me and it feels great. Something as simple as concentrating on the ice chip brought me great joy. My need had been met and someone cared enough about what I needed. I didn't have to do anything except receive it. All these years with Tyler, caused me to stop feeling. That was so dangerous; I knew Tyler was treating me wrong. I trained myself to just ignore what I was feeling, then I could cope. I permitted the abuse to numb me. I normalized the absurdity.

The nurse is right, when and why did I fool myself into believing that Tyler loved me. Beating me was not honoring me. Putting me in an emotional cage was not honoring me, while handcuffing me to his expectations. It was wrong! Somehow, I believed that his obsession was a testament to how much he loved me and equated his control to devotion to us. Now, I realize that I was wrong. It was abuse, mental and physical abuse, period.

I want to rest, so when the nurse comes back, we can talk. I allow my body to rest and close my eyes to savor the feeling of safety. This is the first time in many years that I can let every muscle relax. I don't have to worry about him waking up and beating me just because he thought I was going to make him mad or he had a dream that I left him. This has been a traumatic event and I know that I will need time and professional support to get to a healthy place.

But for now, I greet sleep and security, with a smile and open heart; it saturates my being. Hello sanity and serenity, let's get reacquainted. I am Cassandra and you're welcome to dwell in my spirit and heart.

"Anna"

I sit down at the table and start to read the newspaper.
Mornings are my favorite time of the day. George hasn't joined me
yet, but I know he will be walking in at any moment. I sip my tea and
savor the robust taste, as I search for yard sales in our community.

"Hey, you early bird," George exclaims.

"Good morning," I reply as I circle an ad.

"What's the plan?"

"I've found three yard sales we can check out. Oh, and the
Home and Garden Extravaganza is in the park. We should check it out
and probably get some new plants or seeds."

"It all sounds good to me. I am ready to roll."

This has been the best times of our life. We're retired and
spend most of our time exploring our city. George and I have been
married for forty-four years. He's my soul mate. We do everything
together. We never had kids, so it has always been just the two of us. I
can't even imagine my life without him. It would be like a blizzard
without snow, leaves without a branch, and cookies without milk. Do
you get the point? Yes, I love him in my core.

"Well, it's 7:40, right now. Let's leave about 8."

"Sounds like a plan to me," I remark getting up from the table
and walking over to the sink.

I leave George in the kitchen eating oatmeal and drinking
coffee. He has eaten the same breakfast every morning since we
married, oatmeal with raisins and brown sugar. That's why I love
George so much. He brought stability into my life. When I couldn't
depend on anyone else, George was there for me. Through it all, the
good, bad, stank and ugly.

The phone rings.

"Anna, get the phone."

"Hello"

"Hello, am I speaking with Anna?"

"Yes"

"Good morning, this is Vickie calling from Dr. Emerson's
office. We have the results back from your annual tests that we did

and Dr. Emerson would like for you to come in the office to review them with you."

"Okay,"

"We have a cancellation this morning. Can you come in within the hour?"

"Sure"

"Great, we will see you then, bye."

"Bye"

I sit the phone down on the dresser. My mind is taken over by the echoing sound of what. What is wrong with me? George walks into the bedroom.

"Are you ready?"

"Ah yeah, but we need to stop by Dr. Emerson's office for a few minutes. She wants to talk to me about my test results."

"Why, what's wrong?"

"I don't know," I answer.

"Now Anna bug don't you start worrying. It's probably your cholesterol or something. You know you have been eating a lot of ice cream and not enough of good ol' oatmeal," he says rubbing his stomach.

I don't reply. George walks over to me and gently kisses me.

"Don't you start fretting over nothing. You are healthy and beautiful and you are going to be fine. You know that I'm right about everything."

I nod in agreement and kiss the top of his bald head.

We wait in Dr. Emerson's office for what seems like forever. George walks around the office inspecting every single degree and plaque that hangs from the wall. He nods after each one and gives it his personal seal of approval.

"Well, the good doctor is well educated and should be able to cure what ails you."

Just then the door to the office opens and Dr. Emerson enters with a file in her hand.

"Hello, Mr. and Mrs. Raleigh."

"Hello, Dr. Emerson," George greets her as he looks at her from head to toe and then nods approvingly.

I smile at George and shake my head.

"Mrs. Raleigh, I just want to go over some results with you."

She sits down and opens the file, flips some papers and stops, then flips two more sheets and then looks up at us.

"Dr. Emerson, I told Anna that she was going to be fine."

"Well, let's take a look at this."

"Anna, your cholesterol and blood glucose tests came back normal."

"See, Anna, I told you that you were healthy as an ox," George announces as he pats me on the back.

I can tell he is nervous and is trying to keep calm. I reach over and take his hand and smile at him. He winks.

"Dr. Emerson, please just tell me why I'm here. If it is bad news just give it to me. Seriously, just say it please."
She closes the folder and stares straight at me and George. I breathe deeply and hold it. I release it and then look at the floor.

"The test that we did on the mass in your right breast revealed that it is cancer. We think that we have caught it early and want to start treatment immediately."

"My wife has cancer. What are you saying? Cancer, my Anna has cancer, are you sure? Did I hear that right?"

"Yes, but let me reassure you that I feel that Anna can beat this. She is healthy, otherwise and there are great oncologists in this area. Trust me, we are going to be right here for this journey."

I wait for my mind to react. I wait for the tears to run down my cheeks, they don't. I wait for the scream, it doesn't happen. I wait and wait, but nothing happens, no reaction and no thoughts.

"I am referring you to a cancer treatment clinic. They are one of the best in the country. They will take good care of you and I will be in contact with them to keep up with your treatment plan and progress. Anna, I feel really good about your chances. Mr. Raleigh, I am optimistic that Anna will be fine."

I stand up and pick up my purse. I want to leave.

"Thank you," George says reaching for my hand.

"Vickie will give you all of the referral information and set up the appointment for you. If you need anything, please call the office."

"Sure," I reply.

George and I don't talk on the way home. We are both trying to figure out how we will fit cancer into our lives. I am too busy for cancer. We visit museums, work in our gardens, volunteer at the elementary school, go to wine tastings, and plays. I don't have time for cancer! Our lives are too full and happy for cancer, nope not happening.

"We can beat this, Anna. The doctor even said so," George proclaims as we walk in the house.

"Yeah," I reply and head for our bedroom.

I turn on the television and flip through the channels. There isn't anything on worth watching. I turn off the television and mope to the kitchen, although, I'm not hungry.

"George, I'm gonna go sit on the porch."

"Do you want company?"

"Not right now."

The sun is extremely bright. I watch our next door neighbor throw a ball to his dog. The laughter and the delightful bark of the dog annoys me. How can everyone be so happy? Did anyone care that I was sick? I suppress the urge to run out into the street and stop every car and yell at them. I have cancer and they have no right to act like nothing is wrong. How can life go on the way that it has been? Things have all changed with one little word, cancer. I repeat it over and over again, cancer, cancer, cancer, it doesn't sound right. I spell it, c-a-n-c-e-r.

"Who are you talking to?" asks George.

"Nobody."

"Do you want to go to the park? I bet we can probably still find some bargains at the yard sales. It's not too late."

"Maybe later, I need a hot shower right now."

George nods his head and sits down. I need to relax. One of my methods of relaxation is to stand in the shower. The hot water usually unties my muscles and frees my mind. I start the shower. I light a few peppermint candles and turn on my nature cd. Soon the bathroom is surrounded by the sounds of rolling waves. The smell of peppermint alerts my mind, while hot streams of water roll down my back, inhale deeply and exhale. I adjust the temperature and increase the pressure of the water. I'm trying to drown out the word cancer that is bouncing around through every crevice of my mind. I strain to hear the rolling waves, but all I hear is the word cancer. Listening more intently, c'mon, only hear the crash of the waves. It's not working. I start to bathe. My soapy hand glides effortlessly over my body, except for my right breast. My entire body is covered with soap suds, except my right breast. There it is alone and uncovered, different from the rest of my body. It was as if it didn't belong to me. I fight the urge to touch it.

How could a part of my body betray me? I have done the monthly exams, although not every month, but I didn't miss any mammograms. I watch what I eat, except for my one indulgence, ice cream. I'm careful when I do my exam. I do them just like the nurse taught me. So, why is this happening to me? I follow all of the rules to the letter, how did this happen to me? Of course, it's a mistake. I check my left breast. I even lift my arm and check my arm pit. I check it a second time and it's perfect.

I smile. Now, time to check the right breast, using the exact technique that I have used for many years. I don't feel anything. It feels normal. Then I start to check near the nipple. I stop. There it is, a hard knot. I press harder to make sure that my fingertips aren't deceiving me. They are not. It is there!

My whole body starts to wobble and then I start to cry. I scream! I clutch both of my breasts.

George bursts through the door and snatches back the shower curtain.

"I have cancer!"

I sank to my knees in the tub; the water beating down on me. I can't contain the madness; it punches my soul and demands to be let out. I relent and set it free, in yelling and cry shrieks. I hear the cd player getting louder and louder. George is turning up the volume on the cd player. He climbs in the shower with me, fully clothed and holds me in his arms. I scream until my throat burns and my mind is satisfied.

The remainder of the morning I sit on the porch totally exhausted.

"Anna, let me tell you something," George declares as he gives me a glass of water.

I sip and then sit the glass by my foot and look at George.

"We are stronger than cancer. You are beautiful, but more than that you are courageous. We are going to this treatment center and we are going to beat this, no matter what. We are going to find out what you need and get it for you."

"But what if," my voice breaks.

"There is no what if. We aren't going to play that game. This is an obstacle that we are going to overcome together. Get off this porch and go get your purse."

"I don't feel like going anywhere," vigorously shaking my head in disagreement.

"The lady called from the center. They have an appointment right now and we are leaving now. The sooner we start the better. You don't have a choice, move it! Let's start this fight, champ!"

I look at him with tears in my eyes.

"We've had enough of that so dry those eyes and get going," he nudges me out of the chair. I agree.

We drive to the Cancer Treatment Center. There it is, the word, cancer, mounted on the building for everyone to see. George and I hold hands as we walk through the door. We scan the directory, it's on the third floor. The elevator zooms there. As soon as we get off, we are greeted by a receptionist.

"Good afternoon, please sign in and we will be with you in just a moment."

I sign in and sit next to George. We are both quiet.

"Mrs. Raleigh, I have some forms that you need to fill out and I need to make a copy of your insurance card and license."

She hands me a mountain of papers. They ask me every question in the world. It takes at least twenty minutes to fill them all out. George reviews each form after I finish it. Each one receives a nod of approval. I give the forms back to her. We wait.
Finally, the door opens.

"Hi, Mrs. Raleigh," she says with a gigantic grin.

"Hello, this is my husband, George Raleigh."

"Please to meet the both of you."

"Anna, the doctor will examine you first and then she will meet with you in the conference room. Mr. Raleigh you may wait for her in the conference room."

George hugs me and follows the nurse to the conference room. He turns around and winks at me and I blow him a kiss.

"Hi, Mrs. Raleigh, I'm Dr. Lipton. I just want to examine your breast and then we will do an ultrasound to check out a few more things and you will be back with your husband before you know it."

The examination is painful. I try to read her face, but I can't.

70

She has a slight smile plastered on her face.

"Mrs. Raleigh, have you felt the lump?" she asks as she places her hand on my shoulder.

I nod my head yes, as a tear rolls down my face.

She pats my knee and hands me a tissue, "We are going to do everything in our power to get you back strong and healthy. I will read over your chart again and meet you in the conference room."

As soon as I open the door, George jumps from his seat and hugs me. He is acting like I have been on a long trip.

"Anna, are you okay? What did she say? What is next?"

"Calm down, she will be in here in a minute to talk to us."

George sits next to me and holds my hand. We wait for almost an hour.

"Hello, again Mr. and Mrs. Raleigh."

"You may call us Anna and George."

"Well, Anna and George the good news is that the tumor is small and that it was caught early. Your previous tests show that your lymph nodes are clear and that the cancer has not spread. Also, your lump is close to your areola and from what we can tell so far, it should be easy to remove. We will make an incision next to the areola and remove the lump. Our team of specialists have discussed your treatment and I would like to share that information with you. If at any time you need me to repeat something or you don't understand something, just stop me. We want you to be comfortable with your plan of care."

George and I lean in to concentrate on everything that Dr. Lipton says. After a long discussion I know everything, I need to know. My anxiety is almost gone. Dr. Lipton's optimism invades my mind and for the first time, I didn't equate cancer with death. We say good bye and drive home.

"Anna, how do you feel?"

"Honestly, I'm still scared but not as much as before. I think that I'm going to be alright. With God, you and Dr. Lipton on my side, I think that we can fight this battle."

George holds both of my hands and looks into my eyes. He doesn't say anything for a few seconds. We stand holding each other's gazes and souls.

"We are going to be fine. Let's pray, Creator, we thank you for all blessings. I thank you for Anna and giving her to me as my wife. We ask that you heal Anna's body and that you strengthen us for this battle. We know that you are able to do all things and we have faith that you are going to heal Anna. We believe in you and know that we are more than conquerors through you that strengthen us. Your Word tells us that You were wounded for our transgressions and bruised for our iniquities, and the chastisement of our peace was upon You, and by Your stripes we are healed. We stand on your Word and speak Your Word because there is power when we proclaim the Word. We love you and thank you in advanced for healing Anna, send angels to surround us, we call on your name and declare and decree it done, Amen."

"Amen!" I shout in agreement.

"Now, my Anna Bug, what are we having for dinner?"

"Something healthy," I say with a grin.

Two weeks later Dr. Lipton performs a lumpectomy on my breast. Then I have a treatment course of radiation. They want to make sure that all of the cancer cells are completely gone. A few months later, I stand in the mirror looking at the scar on my breast.

"What are you doing?"

"Just looking at my scar," I answer as I run my finger across it. It's smooth and slightly raised.

"It isn't bad at all," George declares as he walks over to where I am standing.

George removes my hand and bends down and gently kisses the outline of my scar.

"God fought the battle and with our faith we won," George declares as he gives my breast a gentle kiss.

"Jaime"

"Bring me a glass of water and a snack."

"Bae, what kind of snack?"

"I want some cookies and ice cream."

Lester is rummaging through the kitchen drawers. I continue to count the number of condoms in the night stand. Shoot, there are five left. I quickly play back the times we had sex over the last couple of weeks. I keep coming up with six. We started out with twelve condoms, so it should be six left. Lester is coming down the hall. I close the drawer and roll back on my side of the bed and turn my back to the door.

"I know you aren't sleep," he says as he sits on the edge of the bed.

"No, I'm just really tired," I reply as I pull the sheets over my head.

"What's wrong Jaime? I brought you some ice cream and cookies," he informs as he pulls the covers from over my head.

"I will eat it later. Put it on the night stand."

"Okay:

He leans in to kiss me and I pull away. He doesn't try a second time. Instead, he turns on the television. I close my eyes. I'm straining my mind, trying to remember the times we have used condoms. I know one is missing. Now, I'm getting pissed.

"I'm going to take a shower," I announce.

"Can I join you?"

"Not this time," I answer picking up my purse and duffle bag off the floor.

I lock the door and turn on the shower. I frantically search my purse for my phone.

"Hello"

"Hello, Peggy"

"Who is this?"

"It's me, Jaime."

"Why do you sound like you are in a hole? I can barely hear you. Why are you calling me at one something in the morning? Are you alright?" Peggy asks.

"Will you just shut up and listen," I demand in a whisper.

"What, I can barely hear you. What are you saying?"

"Shh, I'm in the bathroom at Lester's house. I don't want him to hear me. I counted our condoms and one is missing."

"Big deal, one condom is missing. Let me get this straight, you called me at one something in the morning to tell me one condom is missing. You woke me up out of some good sleep heifer to tell me about a condom. I am about to hang up on you, bye," Peggy was half serious and half joking.

"No, no wait, I think he is cheating on me. Stop laughing, there isn't anything funny. What should I do?" I ask somewhat irritated with Peggy.

"Get your butt off the phone, take a shower and go to bed. So, what if one condom is missing. If he is messing around with someone, she isn't anything to worry about if he only used one condom," Peggy declared. "Girl, go to sleep."

"I know I should have stayed by myself," I remark still whispering.

"Jaime, please don't start. Drama Queen, go to bed. You probably counted wrong. You know you not good at math. Girl, count them again and then if you are still mad, ask him what happened to it in the morning. All sane people are sleep right now. Go to sleep."

"But wait, he will know I count them, and if he is messing around, I will never find out, because he will buy two boxes and I will never know. Oh no, I gotta go he's knocking on the door."

I throw the phone in the duffle bag, then turn off the shower.

"Jaime, why did you lock the door, open up I've got to use the bathroom," Lester shouts, vigorously twisting the knob.

I slip on my gown and open the door.

"Since when did you start locking the door?"

"Since tonight!"

Lester comes out of the bathroom and looks at me. I'm sitting on the edge of the bed.

"Where is my ice cream?" I ask trying to sound like I'm not annoyed.

"I put it back in the freezer because it was melting," he says getting under the covers.

"Will you go get it for me?"

"Why can't you go get it?"

I stick out my lip and pretend to pout. I can tell he is getting sleepy.

"Fine, I'll get it," Lester says with a huge sigh.

I run around the foot of the bed and open the dresser drawer; I count five condoms. I have proof he's cheating on me. I close the drawer and hurry back on the other side of the bed. I bend down to look under the bed for my shoes. I am not staying over here tonight. I see three condom wrappers on the floor. Tonight, we used two.

"What are you looking for," Lester asks as he sits the bowl of ice cream and cookies on the night stand.

"Why are there three condom wrappers on the floor?"

"If you must know, I unrolled it wrong and I had to use another one."

I feel stupid. I pick up the wrappers and throw them in the garbage. I eat the ice cream and cookies and fall asleep.

I need to call Peggy to let her know that she was right again.

"Hello"

"Hey, Peggy"

Chuckling Peggy asks, "Did you solve the case of the missing condom?"

"Yeah, it was on the floor. He unrolled it wrong and had to use another one."

"I have told you about being paranoid and jumping to conclusions for no apparent reason."

"Yeah, whatever!"

"You need to start listening to me and then you won't have to call me at one in the morning from the bathroom, whispering and acting silly crazy."

"Okay, you've made your point!"

Peggy always told me to stop looking for reasons to distrust Lester. I have been hurt many times. It seems like every man that I become involved with promises me diamonds, but in the end, I'm always left with shards of glass and abandonment. My dad even abandoned me. I am afraid to believe that Lester is any different. I've decided that I must protect my heart. I will never allow myself to become too involved, my heart can't take the pain anymore. I have all

75

of my guards up and they aren't coming down for anyone.

"What are you doing today?" Peggy inquires.

"I want to go bowling with Lester, but I don't want to ask him because I initiated last night."

"There you go again. Why does that even matter? If you want to go bowling, then call him and go bowling. You are creating confusion before it even starts. You need to stop playing games! First, you should have listened to me. I told you that you should not be having sex anyway. That opens up too many other emotions that you can't handle. Why are you being so complicated? You have a lot of work to do on yourself without adding someone else and sex to the mix. Work on Jamie, hint, hint. You need to shut down the sex and focus on building a friendship."

"You think that you know everything. Newsflash to Ms. Know It All Peggy, you don't know everything, and I'm getting sick of your advice," there's a bit of tension in my voice.

"I couldn't agree with you more; I don't know everything but I know you. And I know you will be an old woman, alone and afraid to let anyone in because they may hurt you. You will die an old scared and lonely woman. Oh, I forgot to say miserable old woman! Oh yeah and I am not gonna pick up the phone when you call me, bye!"

She's right. I see the scary picture that she has painted for me. I call Lester and invite him to go bowling. When he picks me up, I smell perfume in the car; it isn't mine. The only perfume I have worn since high school is *Spring Rain*. This is not *Spring Rain!* It smells like old stank roses and menthol rub.

"What woman has been in this car?" I ask staring at Lester.

"What are you talking about?" His face etched in a frown.

I don't say anything.

"Jaime, why are you asking me that? The only other woman that has been in this car is my mom. Don't start, please. I need peace today."

I don't reply. As soon as we get to the bowling alley, I tell Lester to get my shoes because I have to use the restroom. Actually, I'm going to find out if Lester is telling me the truth. I go into a restroom stall and take out my phone and call Lester's mom.

"Hello"

"Hello, Mrs. Hughes, this is Jaime."

"Hi, sweetheart"

"How are you doing?" I ask trying to sound cheery.

"Just fine, thank you."

"I was wondering if Lester was there. He was supposed to pick me up to go bowling and he is late."

"No, he isn't here. I saw him earlier today when he took me to the craft store. He told me he was on his way to pick you up. Hmm, I don't know, I hope nothing bad happened," she sounds worried.

"Wait, Mrs. Hughes here he is right now, sorry to have bothered you."

"Not a problem, have a good time, bye Jaime"

"Bye"

I laugh as I hang up the phone. Why am I acting so silly? I check my makeup and join Lester. We have a fantastic time bowling. I bowl a perfect game. Lester suggests we go to his house to watch a movie. I never knew such simple things could bring such pleasure. I just love being with him, doing ordinary things like laundry and going to the grocery store. I curl up next to him on the couch. The movie starts. The phone rings.

"Hello, of course, can I give you a call later? Perfect, good bye," Lester says and hangs up the phone.

"Who was that on the phone?"

"A girl from work, do you want some chips or popcorn?"

"No," I reply as I move away from him and sit on the floor.

"Why are you sitting down there?" Lester asks as he strokes my hair.

I pull away from his touch and immediately, anger surfaces.

"What is your problem?"

"Ask the girl from work and see if she can answer your question."

I can't believe I just said that. It feels like an out of body experience. I'm thinking that, but my mouth wasn't supposed to say it. It tumbles out, all of my insecurities. Lester looks at me with a puzzled look. I can tell he is trying hard not show his frustration.

"Really, here we go again," he sighs loudly, as he stands to his feet.

I can't help it. I'm going to break up with Lester before he has the chance to break up with me. It is too good to be true. He is just like all the other men. I get up and walk into the bedroom and start gathering my things. I try to hold back the tears, but they rush down my face and rest on my lips. I taste the saltiness as I pinch my lips together. Lester stands in the doorway watching me. I sling my purse across my shoulder and grab my picture off of the dresser. He blocks the doorway.

"Move out the way! Mooove!" I yell.

Lester doesn't move. He just stands there looking at me.

"Move right now!" I shout and try to push my way around him. It's not working. He's too strong for me to push out of the way. I stand there pressing my body against his. You would think I'm on a football field doing tackle drills. I shove and grunt and push. Lester doesn't budge. I can't move him. He just stands in complete silence.

Lester opens his arms and draws me into his embrace. He bends down and whispers in my ear. I struggle to pull away from him, but his grip is too powerful. The picture drops out of my hand and my purse slides off my shoulder.

"Don't sabotage us because you are scared to love. You are the most important person in my life. I don't want anyone else. I am not your father and all of the other men that left you. I am Lester. Jamie, only you can make me smile when I have had a rotten day. You are an incredible woman. You need to believe that. Please believe me; I will never intentionally hurt you. Don't punish me because what other people did to you. What else can I do to show you? Tell me what to do and I will do it. I love you."

I look into his eyes, and they glisten with the truth. A small chip of fear and abandonment that had frozen my heart slowly melts away, as Lester holds me in his arms. He whispers I love only you, over and over in my ear. I weep uncontrollably as I finally realize that Lester means every word that he is saying. The tears reveal the stains of rejection and abandonment that soil my heart. I want to open my heart and let Lester in and kick out the haunting memories of my past relationships. In this moment, I realize I'm not ready. My heart is so messed up and loaded with insecurity. I have a heart full of crap and junk. There's no room for Lester. Matter of fact there isn't any room for anyone.

"Lester, thank you," I say with true gratitude.

He continues to hold me.

"I need time to work on me, some time to get myself together," I announce as I try to shut off the faucet of tears.

"I thought we just did that; I told you I love you."

I look at him, "I know, but you deserve a whole woman not some insecure jacked up girl. I need to figure this out, I have some issues that I need to deal with before I can be happy with you. Trust me, this is not about you. It is all about me and letting go of the past, in order for me to truly love. I'm tired of snooping around and getting mad and feeling like I have to catch you in something. Do you understand what I am trying to say? I mean, I can't keep going on like this. I'm unhappy and I'm stressing you out. I'm stressed and a mess, I am broken."

"Yeah, I get it. Jamie, handle your business. That is why I love you. Does this mean that we can't see each other, or what? How can I help you? You are my friend first, before anything else. I want to help you."

"I don't have all the answers right now, I just know that I am messed up and I don't want to keep being this way. I can't keep up with the foolishness. I need to come to grips with my past and learn to love myself, so I can really love you. Eventually, I want us to be together, but I am not asking you to wait for me. You have to do what is best for you, because I have to do what is best for me. Right now, I am in no condition to be in a relationship. I am glad that I realize that and you just showed me how silly I've been acting. It has to stop. I don't like who I am right now. I need to figure out why I do what I do. I have some serious trust issues. I need to get counseling."

"I hear you, but if you need anything just let me know. I will give you your space and you know where I am. I have so much respect for you right now," Lester says with a smile of admiration.

"Thanks," I reply hugging him and kissing him on the cheek.

I feel so much better, like a weight has been lifted off of me. I want to face my abandonment and trust issues. I'm done ignoring them and letting them run wild, controlling my life and mood. I have been on a rollercoaster and car crash all at the same time, running from relationship to relationship. I will dig up all that toxic waste; I need new soil so some good seeds can grow. I am scared of what I must say out loud to a therapist, but I'm more afraid of what kind of life I will have if I don't deal with it.

Peggy will be proud. If Lester waits for me that's great, but if he can't that's fine. It's not about a man. Wow, for the first time I can say it. Hold it, let me say that again, it's not about a man! I am not on a man hunt, but a Jamie hunt. I need to learn to love me, before I can truly love Lester. This is a journey that will take time and I am not going to put a date on it. My heart will tell me when the time is right, because she won't be shrouded in insecurity, fear, and toxic remembrances that hide the light of promise.

"Rana"

Today is my big day! This day can make me or break me. I dial my mom's number.

"Hello"

"Hey, mom it's me."

"Well, what happened?" she inquires with excitement.

"Nothing, I haven't seen him,"

"How do you feel?" she has uncertainty in her voice.

"I'm cool and calm. I'm ready for this. I've laid the foundation and now it is time to seal the deal."

"Just remember all that I've taught you and don't be stupid. Remember that he is a man and you have all the control, play your cards and handle your business. You set the tone and don't back off," Mom says firmly.

"Thanks, and I'll call you and give you an update, bye mom."

"Work it, Rana," she demands.

I look at myself in the mirror and inhale. I need to put my game face on. I get out the car and walk into the building. I pull my skirt down a little and run my fingers through my hair. I walk quickly to my office and lock my purse in the desk.

"Rana, you still here?" asks Krista.

"Yeah Krista, I have a few more phone calls to make and then I'm leaving. Are you on your way out?"

"Yep, I'll see ya tomorrow. Oh, by the way, I heard that Mr. Westin has selected our new department manager."

"Really," I remark somewhat puzzled.

"I heard that it is Meagan Huntlee. Of course, that is only office gossip, but she did just finish over fifty hours of executive leadership training."

"Good for her," I reply nonchalantly.

"I'm outta here and don't you stay too long."

"Good night," I say with disappointment in my voice.

Whatever, I am not concerned about office gossip, because I have a secret weapon. I don't care that Meagan had taken Mr. Westin's advice and taken those management courses. She is just plain ugly and boring. She wears plaid dresses and skirts that are way below her bony kneecaps. I don't want to even think about those bushy caterpillar eyebrows. Not to mention that slicked back hair bun. She is a fashion nightmare. I may not have book smarts, but I have the perfect body and that will take me anywhere I want to go. It has never let me down and I'm using it to my advantage. Why let a good thing go to waste? Yep, this hot body is my secret weapon, now watch me work.

I take a quick stroll around the office to make sure that everyone is gone. It's all clear. Next stop, restroom, I review every part of myself in the mirror. I love the way the skirt is fitting; it accentuates my tight butt and is short enough to show off my shapely calves. This tight-fitting V neck blouse and the push up bra is giving the perfect cleavage. I am irresistible! Of course, I've worn a blazer all day, but now it is time to take it off. The blazer won't grab Mr. Westin's attention. I take a small tube of petroleum jelly out of the blazer's pocket. I squeeze out a small amount and rub it on my breasts. My cleavage is glistening. I pull my hair around to my nose to smell it. It still smells like my perfume. Hair is an important part of the package. I have luxurious hair; it is soft and has a slight curl to it. I always get compliments on my curl pattern and color. My locks are a beautiful brown with streaks of copper. Most men love to bury their face in my hair and I'm sure Mr. Westin is no exception. I walk back to my office to make sure everyone is gone and to drop off the blazer.

I'm standing in front of the elevator and push the number four. I work for a medical insurance claims company. Our department handles Workers Compensation claims for various companies. I complete data entry, interview clients and a lot of filing, but if given the chance I know that I can run this department. I'm not great when it comes to tests and class situations, but I am smart. Many people in this company think that if you don't have a degree, then you can't move up in the company. I will prove them wrong, especially if I can get Mr. Westin to agree with me. With some body persuasion, I'm sure he will. I am blessed with a body and a mom that taught me how to use it. Trust and believe, I'm doing just that!

I step off the elevator and there is a sense of relief, because Mr. Westin's, secretary, Betty, has left for the day. I knock on his office door.

"Come in"

"Hello, Mr. Westin"

"Hello, Rana how are you doing?" Mr. Westin asks placing his pen down on the desk.

"I'm wonderful. May I sit down?"

"Absolutely, you wanted to talk to me about the managerial position in your department, correct."

"Yes, the office grapevine says that you have already selected someone."

"Never rely on the grapevine," he replies with a slight smile.

Mr. Westin is handsome, so this is going to be enjoyable. Trust me, I've endured bad hygiene and funky breath before, I don't care as long as I get what I want. Mr. Westin is about fifty-five years old with curly black hair. He has a beautiful smile and the whitest teeth that money can buy. His body, well let me just say, he is workout everyday kind of fine. There aren't any blemishes on his olive skin. He's divorced and almost a millionaire. He is fine, oh and rich, let me say that again, fine and rich.

"I'm very interested in that position and I know that I would do a wonderful job," I say confidently. I stare into his eyes. He stares back at me.

"Have you completed the leadership training?"

I knew it, here we go. I lean forward with my hands down to my side and take a deep deliberate breath. I see his eyes drop down, straight to my breasts.

"Actually, I haven't taken the courses, but I am a great leader and I have so much to offer, if you will just give me a chance," I remark with a slight sexy huskiness in my voice.

"There are several people in that department that have applied for the position."

"I don't think they have all the things that I have to offer to you and to this company. I can assure you that I will be the best," I respond looking down at my breasts and then slowly looking back at him. "I'm a very talented young lady and I can show you that." I stand from my seat and lean over the desk and lick my lips.

He looks at me with a puzzled look etched across his face. I walk around the desk and swivel his chair around to face me. He still looks stunned and confused. Wow, guess he is a little slow, not that smart.

"I'm willing to do whatever it takes." I place my hands on the arms of his chair and allow my hair to gently brush against his cheek. He rolls his chair away from me and stares at me. I can tell that he is taking very deep breaths and exhaling slowly. He is trying to gather his composure. I am standing directly in front of him. I am like a tree planted by the water; I am not going to move.

"Mr. Westin, we are both adults. I'm not married and neither are you. I want to prove my loyalty to you and this company. You name it and consider it done. Whatever, you want," I place a strong emphasis on the word whatever.

I step forward and lean down and kiss his forehead; he doesn't roll the chair back. Then I kiss his cheek; he doesn't pull away. I smile. I stand up straight and walk back to the chair and sit. He looks at me. I can tell he is trying to decide what he is going to do. His mind is being logical, but his body is not.

"Timothy, I will be the best that you ever had," I pause, "manager that is."

"Rana, you're smart and it won't take you long to finish the leadership program and then you will be on your way. People will wonder how you got the job without going through the program. I will come under fire and then the rumor mill will start. We don't need that happening. I know you can do it if you apply yourself. Let's just do this the right way, okay. This will not be good for me or you. I am not going to play this game."

I stand up and walk over to the door and lock it; I guess he didn't get it.

"Tim, I'm an excellent worker. Everyone knows that I am smart. Once I get the job, I will go to the classes. You can say that you saw something special in me. You know that I am a natural leader. No one will question you. I will do such a great job that there won't be any reason for anyone to complain."

"I agree with you, but," he was in deep thought.

I interrupt him, "There is no but, except this one," I say slowly rubbing my butt. I lift my skirt and gently roll down my thigh highs and step out of them. I'm about to unbutton my skirt and drop it to the floor, but he stands up from the chair. He stares at me from toe to head; his eyes stop for a moment at my waist.

84

He clears his throat and shakes his head in disbelief.

"Ms. Rana Weldon you are putting me in a very difficult position," he states with a noticeable frown on his face. "Put your thigh high or stockings, whatever you call them, on right now! This is outrageous. Did you think that you were going to walk in here and just seduce me? Do you think that I am that weak and stupid?"

I am not sure if that is a real question or a rhetorical one. Now, I am standing by the door fully dressed and baffled. What is going on?

Mr. Westin shakes his head and instructs me to leave his office immediately.

I walk back to my desk and just sit there with my mind cluttered in confusion and worry. My phone rings, it's mom.

"What took you so long to call me? What happened?"

"Um, I'm just leaving. It took a little longer than I thought."

"Why, what happened?"

"I tried to convince him to go for it. I thought he was going to be enticed and have sex with me. No, he told me to get out of his office. He was very ticked off with me."

"Wait, what, you must have done it all wrong. You had your cleavage thingy going on and you did the hair in his face move, right?"

"Of course, I did all of that, the cleavage and everything, just like we planned and he threw me out the office. Hell, I might even lose my job or something worse than that. What if he sues me or report me to HR for sexual harassment, ugh, can men file a claim? This is not good!"

"Stop talking! Shut up Rana, I told you that you don't leave until the deal is sealed. You should not have let him off the hook! How could you leave it wide open like that? Rana, haven't I told you to handle your business!" she screams into the phone.

"Don't yell at me! It is your fault that I am in this mess," I respond in anger.

"Rana, the job was yours! I taught you better than this. Come up with a strategy, you messed up! Get back in the game and get back up in that office and do damage control."

"Seriously mom, you want me to go back up there! Are you listening to anything that I have told you? Mr. Westin may fire me, period. He may accuse me of sexual harassment, period."

"No, you worry too much. It's about getting twenty-two

thousand more dollars a year and a two-week paid vacation. This is about getting a promotion and you left the job undone. Rana, figure out what you need to do and do it! We need that money!"

"Maybe you are right, but I don't know," I say replaying the incident to see if there is any way I can recover and get back in the game.

"Handle your business," she demands as she hangs up.

Hmm, she might be right.

The next morning, I arrive at work two hours earlier than usual and head straight to Mr. Westin's office. Betty isn't at the desk; I knock on the door, no answer. I open the door and slip inside. His suit jacket is hanging on the back of his chair; I walk over to it, place something in the pocket and leave.

Our department gathers around 10:00 AM and everyone is already congratulating Meagan for being the new manager. I step into the hall to see if Mr. Westin is coming. The elevator doors open and Mr. Westin steps off and looks at me. I can't read his expression; it's blank.

"Good morning," I say looking around to see if anyone else is getting off the elevator.

"How are you?" he replies in a matter-of-fact tone.

"Very fine, but of course you know that already. You may want to check your right jacket pocket before you go in the meeting," I say softly as I walk a few steps away from him to the water fountain. I bend over and pretend to drink. Mr. Westin is eyeing me. He reaches in his pocket and the shock on his face is priceless. He quickly stuffs my white thong from last night back in the pocket.

Everyone is attentive during the meeting. We don't know if he is going to make the announcement at the end or beginning of the meeting.

The fifteen of us are locked on his mouth trying to ready ourselves for the announcement. I look over at Meagan and she is jotting down everything that Mr. Westin says. She is a meticulous note taker. I guess she dressed up for her big promotion. Instead of wearing her usual plaids, she is wearing a dress with red stripes. Her hair is pulled into a low left side ponytail. A ponytail vs. the granny bun, I can't decide which is more hideous. She is straight pitiful; even if you gave her a makeover, she wouldn't look any better, poor girl.

86

"I guess I will announce what all of you have been waiting to hear. I received four resumes and applications for the position of department manager. I was impressed by all of them, to say the least. I am looking for a person willing to do whatever it takes to succeed, and someone that can take this department to a new level and go the extra mile. This department needs a natural leader. The person that has these qualities is Ms. Megan Huntlee! I look forward to her making this department even better and building the capacity of this team."

Meagan is overjoyed and everyone is hugging her.

What, I am flabbergasted! That trick from this morning was supposed to let him know that I am not scared and that I will do anything to succeed. Why didn't he change his mind? I don't care who sees me talking to him. I immediately follow him to the elevator. He needs to explain his decision.

"Excuse me, but what just happened in there? That job is mine; I don't understand why you picked her. Last night, was about letting you know that I am willing to do anything for this company and for you; am I missing something? Wait, oh I got it now, you like the homely type or are you gay?"

Mr. Westin is just looking at me, and then he finally replies, "Rana, no I don't like the homely type and no I didn't have sex with her. Not that my personal life is any of your business, and no I'm not gay. This is about business. How can I trust you to run a department when you don't even trust yourself? Leaders must have confidence in themselves and their skill set."

"What are you talking about? I am confident."

"You don't trust your brain and knowledge; you trust your body. You didn't have enough confidence in yourself to even try to take the classes. I am not going to appoint people to lead my departments when they cannot even lead themselves. Is your plan to sleep your way to the top? If so, let me just say that is not smart and you need to come up with another career plan. Also, to be clear, you won't be sleeping in my bed. That is not how I select my team members or leaders. You put me and yourself in an awkward position last night. Listen, Rana, I can fire you for many reasons, but I won't. I am going to extend grace to you."

He reaches in his pocket and pulls out my thong, "You may want this. I don't have any use for it and don't ever come to my office and try me again. If I even think that you are approaching any other team members, the way you approached me, I will take action against you. Also, I suggest you support your new manager. I will not tolerate any insubordination."

I snatch the thong from him. I am dumbfounded. That was my career plan, now what am I going to do? Even more concerning than that, what am I going to tell mom?

"June"

I walk through the halls as quietly as possible. No one has trays outside their doors. I look at my watch. It is 10:15 P.M. I get back on the elevator and press the number five. There are five more floors to go and I am starting to get anxious. The elevator stops and I get off, and take a quick glance down the hall. Great, I spot two trays sitting on the floor. I'm glad that no one else is in the hall. I tiptoe to the trays and lift the silver dome. There is a half-eaten baked potato, about seven string beans and a drumstick that someone had taken a bite out of. I take the napkins out of my purse and wrap up the food. I sip from the glass; it's ginger ale. I hear the elevator chime and the doors open. I pretend that I'm looking for my room key. The couple passes by and don't even seem to notice that I'm standing there. I wait a few seconds and walk quickly to the second tray which is a few feet away. I look around and again lift the silver dome off the plate. It is empty. I lift the silver dome off the second plate and discover an entire hamburger meal. Once again, I take more napkins out of the purse and wrap up the hamburger and fries. I pick up the dill pickle spear and shove it in my mouth. It's crunchy and satisfying. There are a few ketchup packets. I get back on the elevator and then look at my watch. I have been gone for an hour. When I reach the lobby, I dart to the side door exit. I don't want to be spotted by the front desk attendant. I sprint to the car and get inside.

"Mommie, what took ya so long," Davey asks as he gets up off the back floor of the car.

"Don't ask so many questions and shut up," Luke remarks hitting Davey in the back of the head.

"Stop it, and get quiet," I say as I take the wrapped food from my purse. I place them on the front passenger seat. I carefully unwrap the food, making sure none of it spills.

"Davey, what do you want, hamburger or chicken?"

"Burger, burger, burger!" Davey shouts.

I give each one of them a wet nap to wash their hands. I use a knife that's under the seat to cut the burger in half, then equally divide the fries. I lean across the seat and place the food in my sons' laps. I give Luke the ketchup packets and he squirts their fries with ketchup. They eat in silence. I watch them as they slowly chew the burger, as if they are trying to make it last as long as possible. I turn back around and bite the drumstick. It is cold and dry. I vaguely taste the lemon pepper seasoning. This is the first food that I have eaten all day, except the pickle. My biggest concern is my children. We have been living in our car for almost two months, after being evicted from our apartment. This car is home sweet home.

After my husband died unexpectedly from a heart attack, I could not make ends meet. We could only afford a five thousand dollar life insurance policy and after his cremation, there was only two thousand dollars left. It just wasn't enough. Needless to say, my minimum wage job could not keep us a float. I went to a shelter, but they refuse to allow me and my boys to live together. Luke is eleven and couldn't be in close sleeping proximity to women and girls, a stupid rule. There was no room in any other shelter. A counselor suggested that I give up custody to the state until I get on my feet. That wasn't an option for me. I was scared that they were going to take my sons away from me, so I left.

I reach on the floor and get the gallon of water and take deep gulps. I hand the jug to Luke and he sips the water.

"Don't drink it all from me," whines Davey.

"It's enough for you, so shut up," Luke remarks handing the jug to Davey.

"You are making me spill the water!" yells Davey.

"You did it yourself, you big cry baby!"

"I'm not a baby! I'm six years old," screams Davey.

"Boys, please settle down," I plead.

"Ma, I'm still hungry," Luke announces licking the ketchup off of his napkin.

"Me too, Ma, I'm hungry too," echoes Davey.

"No you not, you just copying off of me!" Luke says as he shoves Davey.

"Luke, please don't aggravate him. You're eleven years old and I need you to act better than this, please. I need you to be a good big brother, please just be nice."

"Yes Ma'am"

I look in my purse. I only have four dollars and I need that

90

money to get gas. I can't deny my babies their basic need of food.

"I'll be back," I take two dollars out of my purse. "Get down on the floor and don't get up until I come back. Davey you do what Luke tells you to do and no talking."

The boys take their positions on the car's floor and I get out and lock the door. I walk back to the hotel's side door and pull on the handle. It's locked. Crap, what I am thinking, I already know you can't open that door without a room key. Going through the lobby is a risk. I stand by the door praying and trying to figure out what to do. I tap on the glass door. A man with a suitcase is getting off the elevator. I motion for him to come open the door; he does.

"Thanks, I left my key in the room and I didn't want to walk all the way around to the front. You know it's been one of those days," I say throwing my hands up in the air to show my frustration and trying not to look suspicious.

"I know what you mean, I have an emergency at home and I'm on my way to the airport right now," he says, "gosh darn it, speaking of keys, I've left my house keys in the room. Now, I've got to go back up and get them," he says with agitation.

We both get on the elevator. He presses the number seven and looks at me.

"What floor?" he asks.

"Same as you, seven," I remark looking at the lit number. "I hope all goes well for you."

"Thanks, I wish I was on my way to sleep instead of to the airport," he shakes his head.

"I'm sure," I respond and smile at him.

The elevator doors open. I step off first and say goodnight. I wait to see which room he goes to. I pretend to go in the opposite direction. His room is at the end of the hall, next to the stairwell. I turn around and sprint down the hall as soon as I see him go into the room. I hurry to the stairwell and open the door and step inside. My heart is exploding inside my chest. I try to quiet the heaving sound that is shooting from my mouth. I struggle to catch my breath. I hold the door open to peep through it. I hope that no one is paying attention to the cameras. Please hurry up, I mumble to myself. Then his door opens and he walks out and heads straight to the elevator. He doesn't even wait to see if the door to his room closes. I dash from the stairwell and stick my foot in his room's door, a second before it closes. I dive in the room and fall on the floor. Suddenly, my mind yells, what are you doing? My heart is racing even more and my breathing is extremely rapid. I've urinated a little because of all of the jumping and running. I stand up in the darkness, still trying to regulate my breathing. After a few minutes, I flip on the lamp and look around the room. There are two queen size beds; one of them is unmade. My eyes immediately zoom over to the desk. There is a fruit basket. It has three bananas, a Granny Smith apple, a pineapple and a jar of honey. I grab the basket. I look around the room to see if there is anything else that I can take. Wait a minute, he's not coming back. I smile. I sit the fruit basket back on the desk. I open the door and look in the hall; it's empty. I take the two dollars out of my pocket and crumple them up and stick them in between the door. I pray that the door doesn't shut all the way, when I let go. It doesn't. I walk down the steps to the first floor and make my way down the hall to the side door. Opening the door, I stare at the car, hoping to see one of my sons looking back at me. Then, I remember, I told them to get on the floor and not to get up until I unlock the car door. Several seconds pass and I don't see any movement in the car. I can't stand here wishing that they look up and see me. Time is of the essence. I wedge my sneaker in the door. Then, walk as quickly as I can to the car. Davey and Luke pop up off the floor, as soon as they hear the lock click.

"Hey, Mommie where's my snack?"

"Davey, give Mommie her purse and boys, put your shoes back on, hurry up."

"Why, Mommie where are we going?"

"It's a surprise, but I need you to be very quiet and to do exactly what I tell you to do."

The boys put on their shoes and wait for more instructions.

"Listen to me, we are going inside the hotel. Don't talk and if anyone stops us, let me answer all of the questions. I need you to walk fast and to be as quiet as you can. This is very important."

The boys get out of the car and I hold Davey's hand.

"Mommie, where is your shoe?" Davey asks.

"She said be quiet," Luke says annoyed with Davey

"No more talking," I say decisively to the both of them. When we reach the door, Davey looks at my shoe stuck in the door. He is

92

about to ask me a question.

"Shh," I say and bend down and pick up the shoe.

"Mommie, you didn't tie your shoe lace," Davey whispers pointing at my shoe.

"It's okay." I whisper back and walk quickly to the end of the hall to the stairwell. We walk up the stairs to the seventh floor.

"C'mon guys," I murmur motioning to them.

"Look, Mommie, someone left money in the door."

I push the door and we walk inside. Davey runs and jumps on the bed.

"Mommie, can I sleep in this bed tonight?"

"Yes," I respond with a sense of relief that we made it. "Luke you can eat any of that fruit that you want."

"Thanks Mom," he grabs a banana.

"Davey, do you want to take a bath?"

"Yeah," he shouts as he runs to me to give me a hug.

I run a warm bath for Davey. I pour some shampoo under the running water to make bubbles. Soon, the tub fills with warm water and white floating foam.

"Yippee, bubbles!" Davey yells as he pulls off his clothes.

I walk out the bathroom and take the remote off of the TV and playfully toss it to Luke.

"You get to watch whatever you want."

I remove the comment card off the desk and read it. He had left a ten dollar bill for the housekeeper. I take the ten dollars and put it in my pocket. Then I straighten out the two dollar bills and place them on top of the comment card for the housekeeper. I got to look out for my kids, sorry.

I give Davey a bath and then make another bubble bath for Luke. Within the hour they are asleep. They sleep in only their underwear. They look so comfortable. Luke has enough room to stretch out and be comfortable; for one night he doesn't have to sleep in the back seat.

Davey usually sleeps reclined back in the passenger's seat, while I sleep next to him in the driver's seat. I kneel beside the bed and stare at them. I must find a way out. I turn off the TV and walk in the bathroom to take a shower. It feels good to take a real shower and not to rinse off in the local fast food restaurant's sink. I linger in the shower for a long time. Finally, getting out, I wrap myself in the terry cloth robe. It is soft and comfortable. I'm thankful that I met the man in the hall; he will never know how much I appreciate him. He is a blessing to me and my sons. Thank you God, for this blessing.

Reclining on the bed, pondering what's the next move, with only twelve dollars. I'm exhausted and need a good night's sleep, but I need to figure out a plan. It is already midnight and I know the housekeeper will clean this room first, since the man has checked out. I pick up the phone and then put it back down. There is no one to call. I was a foster kid. My husband's family was pretty much nonexistent, but he did have a sister. Again, I pick up the phone. I hope that no one would notice that a call was being placed from this room. I pray and dial the number. This will be the only time that I am able to use a free phone; it was late but my boys depend on me.

"Yeah," answers a sleepy voice.

"Hi, sorry to call so late, but may I speak to Evelyn."

"Yeah, it's me, who this?"

"It's June."

"June, who?"

"It's June, Big Luke's wife. Your brother's wife." We talked briefly at Big Luke's memorial, but that conversation is a blur.

"Yeah, sorry June I didn't catch your voice. What's wrong? The boys alright? Why ya callin?"

"I was wondering if I could come by to see you tomorrow?"

"Uh, sure do you know where I live?"

"Yes, I've been there a few times with Big Luke."

"How's Lil Luke and Davey?"

"Just fine, thanks for asking. I will bring them with me."

"Good then, see you tomorrow."

"Okay and sorry for calling so late," I say apologetically.

"No problem," she replies.

I set the clock for 5:15 in the morning and turn out the light. The bed caresses every part of my body. I hug the pillow. I miss my husband. There is a yearning for him that I can't even express with words. Sometimes the void is so painful, that it feels like I won't find anything worthy of filling it. It feels raw. The tears roll freely down my face. I need to hear Big Luke's voice to reassure me that we are going to be fine. I long for him to hug me and there have been times

94

that I have strained to remember what his embrace feels like to my spirit. There is a heaviness that sits on each shoulder of the essence of me. Each day is a struggle to get moving; my children are the life sustaining motivation. I have been in survivor mode for the last few weeks, but sometimes the grief overpowers me and punches the life out of my heart. Tonight, the grief wins and my body trembles as I cry myself to sleep.

Beep, Beep, I jump up and turn off the alarm clock. I look over at Luke and Davey. They are still asleep. I take a few moments to gather my thoughts. I look at the clothes on the air conditioning unit; I rinsed them out last night.

I iron them to remove the last trace of dampness and place them across the chair. Looking around the bathroom, I decide to take the washcloths, towels, soap and lotion. I place them in the large plastic bag that I had taken out of the closet. There is barely any room for the pineapple and jar of honey, but I can't leave them, so in the bag they go. It's 5:45 A.M. There is a free breakfast buffet in the lobby that starts at 6. I gently wake the boys with a kiss.

"Morning Mommie," Davey says as he stretches.

"Get dress, and remember to be quiet."

Davey smiles at me and pretends to zip his mouth and throw away the key. We all dress and walk to the lobby. I am surprised to see that it is packed with boys around Luke's age. They're wearing soccer uniforms and carrying backpacks and luggage. The breakfast buffet is set up across from the lobby. The front desk attendants are so busy checking out the soccer team that no one notices us. We walk over to the food.

"Oh Mommie, can I have cereal?"

"Yes Davey, but we are going to take it with us."

Luke is staring at the boys.

"Luke hon, grab some cereal and I'll get some cartons of milk," I say quietly.

He picks up several small boxes of assorted cereal. I open the plastic bag and he drop them inside. I grab five small cartons of milk and drop them in my purse. Two of the soccer boys are looking at us. I don't want to draw any more attention to us. I grab a couple of muffins and tell the boys it's time to go. We walk out of the lobby and to the car. Once we are inside, I prepare the boys' cereal and I eat the

95

muffins with honey. We finish our breakfast and I drive to the nearest gas station. I put seven dollars of gas in the car, the needle is barely above E.

"Boys, we are going to visit your Auntie Evelyn. I want you to be on your best behavior and don't say anything, let me do all the talking. You say hi to her and that is it. You hear me?"

"Mommie, I won't say one word. I will be super-duper quiet," Davey remarks grinning at me and crossing his fingers.

It takes about 25 minutes to get there. I've decided I am just going to tell her the truth. The house looks decent from the outside. Actually, I am not concerned about how it looks; my boys need somewhere to live. I knock on the door; my stomach is swirling. Evelyn opens the door and steps aside for us to walk in.

"Have a seat," she says pointing to a green sofa.

"Ev, I'm going to get right to the point. I need somewhere to live for a few months. I need help to get on my feet," my voice cracks.

"June, what's going on with ya?" she questions with her overly arched brows slightly lifting.

I can't speak. Grief and exasperation are all tied up in my throat and my words can't squeeze by them.

"We been livin' in the car, but last night we stayed in a hotel and I took a big bubble bath," Davey blurts out.

"Shut up," Luke says fearfully to Davey.

"June, is this true?"

I nod my head yes, "When Big Luke died, I just couldn't do it. I am just desperate. We can't go to the shelter. You are the only person. I. I."

Evelyn puts up her hands, "Hold on, no need to go spreadin' ya business. You don't owe me and nobody else no explanation. You shoulda called me sooner. You my brother's family, so that means we family. Y'all stay right here. It's settled. Big Luke wouldn't have it any other way. You are my kin folk."

"This means so much to me," I tearfully reply.

"My brother wouldn't be able to rest in peace if I turn y'all away. You can stay right here. Then when you and the boys ready you can get your own place. But, no need to rush, I can use the company. I got two extra bedrooms and we'll have to share a bathroom. It ain't no mansion or nothing, but it's home. Let me show you to your rooms.

June, the boys can share and you can have your own room for a tad bit of privacy. This here is your home now."

"Yippee," Davey yells and runs to hug Evelyn.

She smiles, "Hey there buddy," and then tousles Luke's hair. Luke smiles at his aunt and immediately I see the family resemblance.

Watching my sons smile and the laughter from Evelyn, causes relief to rush throughout my body.

"Once you guys bring in your stuff, let's go to HouseMart to pick out some things to decorate your rooms and then let's go to the grocery store. I am gonna cook a great big ol celebration meal for y'all" Evelyn says with genuine love.

"Thanks Ev, I am so glad I called you."

She opens her arms and so do I, we stand, holding each other and I feel the energy of kindness and compassion.